Praise for
The Winter Seeking

"A touching story of a woman's search for her place in the world, as only Vinita Hampton Wright can tell it."

—PHILIP GULLEY, author of the Harmony series

"Spiritual without being sentimental, *The Winter Seeking* is the perfect short read on a cold Christmassy night. I know that curling up with this novella will now be part of my annual Yuletide tradition."

—LAUREN WINNER, author of *Girl Meets God* and *Mudhouse Sabbath*

"Vinita Hampton Wright covers a lot of emotional ground in her novella *The Winter Seeking*. This story evocatively depicts a refreshing and inspiring journey to faith that the reader shares alongside Jana. As a songwriter, I am always moved by fresh perspectives, and this story truly delivers a new glimpse into the nativity."

—JILL PAQUETTE, singer and songwriter

"My Christmas shopping problems have been solved! I will be getting copies of *The Winter Seeking* for all my family, friends, and spiritual companions. This warm and deftly written novella gives hope to those of us who hold to our faith in these uncertain times. *The Winter Seeking* serves as an easily opened door to the world of Christian meditation, as well as being an entertaining and heartwarming reading experience. Those of us who have enjoyed Vinita Wright's other novels are not surprised to see her characters come to life on the page and enrich our lives. I didn't want this novella to end."

—LYN HOLLEY DOUCET, author of *Water from Stones* and *A Healing Walk with St. Ignatius;* spiritual director, The Emmaus Center of Spiritual Direction, Our Lady of the Oaks, Grand Coteau, Louisiana

THE WINTER
SEEKING

VINITA HAMPTON WRIGHT

THE WINTER
SEEKING

A NOVELLA

WATERBROOK
PRESS

THE WINTER SEEKING
PUBLISHED BY WATERBROOK PRESS
2375 Telstar Drive, Suite 160
Colorado Springs, Colorado 80920
A division of Random House, Inc.

Scripture quotations are taken from *The Holy Bible, New Living Translation,* copyright © 1996. Used by permission of Tyndale House Publishers, Inc., Wheaton, Illinois 60189. All rights reserved.

The characters and events in this book are fictional, and any resemblance to actual persons or events is coincidental.

ISBN 1-57856-827-7

Library of Congress Cataloging-in-Publication Data
Wright, Vinita Hampton, 1958–
    The winter seeking : a novella / Vinita Hampton Wright.—1st ed.
    ISBN 1-57856-827-7
    1. Adult children of divorced parents—Fiction. 2. Parent and adult child—Fiction. 3. Mothers and daughters—Fiction. 4. Cancer—Patients—Fiction.
I. Title.
    PS3573.R548W56 2003
    813'.54—dc21
                                                                    2003011830

Printed in the United States of America
2003—First Edition

10 9 8 7 6 5 4 3 2 1

*To every young woman
who needs company on the journey*

ACKNOWLEDGMENTS

Thanks to Kathryn Helmers, my agent, for nudging me to try a project like this. Thanks to Dudley Delffs, my editor, for his enthusiasm and insight. Thanks to the whole WaterBrook team for making this book work so well. And thanks to the pilgrims, spanning the centuries, who have brought imagination and Scripture together through *lectio divina*.

THE JOURNEY

*S*itting in a stalled car during a blizzard did not enhance Jana's sense of independence. She regarded herself in the rearview mirror. "This is so typical," she said. "Just as I'm making my escape." She could barely see ten yards in any direction. Snowflakes the size of feathers swirled by the millions and then drifted crazily to earth, as if a pillow fight were taking place far above.

She calculated that she was about three miles off the interstate, which she had left by her own decision. She'd thought that moving *somewhere* would be better than staying on the parking lot that was I-25. Reports said a tractor-trailer had jackknifed miles ahead. Whatever had happened, the southbound traffic was stopped as far as Jana could see. She had pulled out the map and seen that the exit she'd just passed hooked up to a highway that could, given some connections, get her to eastbound I-40 eventually. So she'd nosed out of line and taken the shoulder back to the exit.

But state highways were not the first priority for snowplows, and, even loaded down with a large suitcase and boxes of books, the little Dodge had slid off the road, making a frightening *clunk* as its front axle hit something metal and immovable. In a few seconds' time Jana was facing not the road but a sloping pasture, while on the radio Judy Collins broke into song—an a cappella version of "I'll Be Home for Christmas." The car's engine had died on impact, and the lone soprano voice rang out with sudden force into the silence.

Jana felt compelled to comment: "I hate holidays. My life would work just fine if it weren't for holidays."

She had just survived Thanksgiving with Dad and his wife. Until a few moments ago, she had been gratefully alone and headed across the country, toward Christmas. She wasn't especially looking forward to Christmas either, but the three-day drive that stretched between the two holidays had become a reward of sorts, long miles to herself in the middle of a season that imposed upon her its lame music and impossible expectations.

Judy was singing plaintively for snow and mistletoe and "presents on the tree..." Jana shut off the radio and tried to restart the engine. It came to life, but the car wouldn't budge backward or forward. Too much snow, or something major broken underneath.

She looked at her cell phone, which was fully charged, imagined Barbra answering the call back at Dad's place. Barbra's face would come alive with concern as Jana described her situation. Barbra's was not the face Jana wanted to imagine, so she called AAA instead. It didn't matter, because the phone wasn't getting a signal.

Well. She could be stuck here for hours. She wrapped her

scarf around her head and pulled up the hood of her parka before stepping out into the storm. A brief examination of the car didn't show her anything; it was in snow up to the floorboard. After packing CDs and their player and her new ski sweater out of sight in the trunk, she locked up and headed back toward the interstate on foot.

Either she didn't pass any houses, or the snowstorm prevented her from seeing them. The temperature had dropped, and panic began to wiggle into her thoughts as she trudged through drifts and fought the wind. *Maybe I should have stayed with the car. It couldn't be more than a few miles, could it?* She did her best to look up through the veil of white. Ahead of her, light poles and power lines stitched a ragged seam toward the horizon. At least they could show her where the road was, and the road would get her somewhere.

She walked with her eyes nearly shut because the snow was blowing into her face. She couldn't help but remember a more gentle snowfall she'd observed just a few days ago at Dad's place. From her bedroom, which still smelled of fresh lumber, she'd looked through the large window that faced the woods and wished she could find more joy in the white-flocked pines. She wished that the peacefulness of snow and the leisure of the holiday were taking place somewhere else, not in this fully loaded A-frame on six acres in the Rockies. It wasn't home, just Dad's place—and Barbra's.

Barbra was nice enough, but she was one of those things that were not supposed to happen. Decent people found a way to live out their commitments. A considerate person did not reinvent himself at age forty-six by acquiring a new home, a new business, and a new wife and leaving the first life and wife behind. Supposedly, Dad did not leave Jana behind. He built her a nice room, after all.

Now all she wanted to do was get to Atlanta and Mom, and not even for the sake of Christmas. Mom had bigger concerns. Her last letter had sounded hopeful—the chemo seemed to have done its job, and now there were radiation treatments to endure. But all this was good news.

Jana looked up again, away from her feet and into the icy wind. She wasn't sure, but maybe that was a gas station or restaurant coming up. Large rectangular forms loomed in a cluster, and thin bluish lights rimmed what looked like the front of a building.

It was a small truck stop, toasty and well worn, its floor smeared with tracked-in mud and snow. Jana felt that she had walked into a movie from thirty years ago as she glanced along the snack bar at men in winter jumpsuits hovering over coffee and plates of meat loaf. One waitress, fortyish, worked behind the counter, and another, younger woman checked the tables and booths. A skinny man wearing a stocking cap sat at a separate counter near the door, where customers paid for gas or items from the few aisles of merchandise. Jana walked up to him.

"Could I use your phone to call triple A?"

Without looking up, he motioned to a pay phone next to the shelves of motor oil. She used her calling card and got through to some office and the voice of a flustered dispatcher. When Jana described her situation, a second opinion was called for at the other end of the line. After a minute or two, the dispatcher picked up the phone again.

"Ma'am, we can get somebody out there in about four hours."

"Four hours?!"

"It's a snowstorm, and all our trucks are out. You're on the list, and we'll get somebody there as soon as we can."

She plopped into a booth at the window. The snow was coming down as thick as ever. She ordered coffee and chocolate cake and tried to consume them slowly. *Four hours to sit here.* She opened the small backpack that served as a purse, hoping she'd brought something useful—and regretting that she'd left her music behind. Her magazines were in the car too. The paperback she'd been reading was the last thing she'd thrown into the backseat that morning. Her journal, at least, was at the bottom of the bag, always with her. She put it on the table, then decided to just clean out the bag. She had nothing better to do, right? An address book and week-by-week calendar, a little pack of tissue, cough drops, the ever-present bottle of ibuprofen, hand lotion, her makeup bag, and her billfold. The billfold bulged—not with money, unfortunately, but with receipts and various notes to herself. This could occupy a half-hour at least. She emptied the billfold and spread out the mess in front of her.

In the midst of ATM receipts and folded-up Post-its, two ticket stubs lay before her. From the Ferris wheel and the Imax theater on Navy Pier back in Chicago. That glorious late-summer day, one of her last pleasant days with Gary.

"Oh, I thought I got rid of all this." Their breakup was almost two months behind her now, but memories of Gary still flashed by with no warning. All it took was for a particular song to come on the radio or for Jana to pass a certain restaurant or for old ticket stubs to tumble out of hiding.

He would be the perfect companion for today's troubles. He'd be putting quarters in the old jukebox over there and telling her not to worry. Gary wasn't the worrying sort. He wasn't the plan-ahead sort either…or the long-term commitment sort. Gary was excellent in areas of having fun and spending too much money. In fact, Jana remembered that he still owed her forty dollars. She gulped coffee and glared at the snow.

Maybe she should swear off men of all kinds. They were just defective somehow—like cars that are built with some glitch and must be recalled. Gary was wonderful in some ways but not enough in the ways that counted most.

And Dad was acting out his midlife crisis in a most unoriginal way. He used a lot of group-therapy talk these days. (Why not? He'd met Barbra in Denver at some conference about reclaiming life's positive energy.) With great intensity he'd explained to Jana about the past hurts and invalidated dreams that had crippled him until now. Yet he seemed to forget with ease that he had lived his entire life in Chicago and been married to Jana's mother for twenty-two years.

Now Jana had lived as many years as her parents' marriage had lasted. Her father would do what he wanted to do. And hardly a year after he left, a mammogram revealed a growth in Mom's left breast, and the biopsy confirmed it as malignant. So she had moved to Atlanta to live with her older sister and get treatments at nearby Emory University Hospital. Meanwhile, Jana, who had graduated back in the spring, kept looking for a job but without much luck. She remained alone in the Chicago apartment she and Mom had shared after the divorce and before the cancer appeared.

So when both parents had left you, you'd broken up with your boyfriend, and you had no job or money, well of course the thing to do was go have a Happy Thanksgiving and then top that off with a Merry Christmas.

During the next three hours, an assortment of people gathered at the truck stop and slowly filled the tables and booths. Jana heard phrases here and there, about "zero visibility" and "sheet of ice"—enough to assure her that she might just spend the rest of her life right here, an anonymous, carless young woman. After a while, the waitress came over and leaned down to speak quietly. "I've got a huge pot of chili. Would you like a bowl on the house?"

Jana didn't know what to say.

"Hon, you're gonna be here a while."

"The roads are that bad?"

The waitress straightened up and nodded. She indicated some men at a nearby table. "When Harvey parks his rig to sit it out, you know it's bad." Her nametag read "Beverly."

"Chili sounds good. Thanks."

Beverly headed back toward the kitchen. The woman's sudden kindness made Jana feel weepy. She swallowed the tears and told herself not to get emotional. She was just tired—that was all. She opened the journal and pulled out the Thanksgiving card Mom had sent from Atlanta. It was a rich gold foil with raised burnt-orange and crimson leaves gleaming on its surface. Inside, Mom had drawn little Christmas angels and holly branches next to the words "Can't wait to have you here for Christmas! Love & prayers, Mom."

Love & prayers. Jana touched one happy angel. Mom talked more about prayer these days. She made every next step with a prayer—that the treatments would work, that she wouldn't throw up too much, that the insurance company wouldn't make all this more difficult.

Opposite Mom's handwriting was someone else's. "Dear Mary Georgianna, It will be so good to see you! May the Lord bless your Thanksgiving. Love, Aunt Cheryl."

Ah yes, for the duration of her Atlanta stay she would once again be Mary Georgianna. She'd gone by Jana since ninth grade, and Mom hadn't called her by her full name in years. But her southern relatives saw her so rarely that she remained in their minds sweet little Mary Georgianna.

I'm making a pilgrimage from New Age freaks to Holy Rollers. Aunt Cheryl's reference to "the Lord" was not a mere holiday sentiment. Mom's Atlanta relatives were very tight with "the Lord." Jana wasn't sure which would be more un-comfortable, seeing Mom sick or being evangelized by Aunt Cheryl.

A huge bowl of chili appeared in front of her, a plate of corn muffins next to it. By the time Jana looked up, Beverly was at another table. The smell of the food hit Jana, and her stomach resounded with growls loud enough to be heard by the family in the next booth. The chili tasted better than any-thing she'd eaten in days. Thanksgiving dinner did not count. Barbra was something of a gourmet cook, and Thanksgiving dinner had been right out of *Bon Appétit.* But the aromas of turkey and dressing seemed horribly misplaced in a new home with a stepmother and a father trying too hard to be cheerful and chummy.

Jana paged through her journal now, bored with the wait but not yet willing to spend money on magazines. She read the latest entry first.

So we're at the dinner table, a couple of days after Thanksgiving, Barbra all perfect with her homemade bread and miso soup. And Dad launches into this monologue about his business partner, John. Repeats verbatim some phone conversation they had sometime this afternoon. Dad is all hyper about the way John said something or how he's been acting lately—I don't know, it seemed pretty minor to me. But Dad is agonizing over this conversation, going on about how it "impacted" him and how he should probably review their written agreement.

And then I notice the expression on Barbra's face—there's all this empathy taking over—and I remember seeing that expression before. On Mom's face. Dad's about to change his life one more time by splitting with his business partner, and Barbra will stick by him, and I'm thinking, How many times did Mom stick by him? Like, how many jobs has he had, and how many major overhauls has he been through?

This is my problem: My father has never become a grownup. It's hard to stay mad at him; I really don't think he can help it. The guy has no anchor at all.

She closed the journal and walked over to the magazine rack, bought a magazine about Western décor, and spent the next hour immersed in make-believe remodeling issues.

She'd walked into the truck stop at half past two. At seven, a wrecker pulled up, its driver looking as weary as Jana felt. Beverly nodded good-bye as Jana bundled up and left a five-dollar tip, the least she could do considering that she'd been sitting there all afternoon and evening, consuming food and drink, most of it for free.

The snow had let up, but night had fallen. The only thing that kept Jana alert was the cold that seized her between the warm café and the truck cab. They made their way down the road and found the car. When Stan, the driver, hauled it out of the ditch, Jana couldn't tell if anything was seriously wrong or not. Stan fastened up the car and jumped into the cab. He radioed the dispatcher without saying anything to Jana.

Finally she asked, "Do you think I can drive it?"

"Maybe. Front end's out of line. You jammed it against the culvert."

"But I can drive it."

"How far you goin'?"

"Atlanta."

He laughed and shook his head. "That's a long way to wobble. It shouldn't be too complicated to get the alignment fixed." He looked at her for the first time. He appeared older than her dad, his face chapped from being out in the weather. His dark curly hair was cut close and sprinkled with gray. "You a college student?"

"I was. Now I'm unemployed." She laughed then. "On my way to spend Christmas with my mom."

"You live here?"

"My dad does. I live in Chicago."

"So you're doin' a bit of driving, huh?"

"Yeah, I like to drive." *I like knowing I can escape at will.* "Usually."

Stan left her and the car at a larger truck stop, back in Pueblo. Of course the garage was closed. Jana took one look at yet another café, this one larger and brighter, and felt so exhausted and sad that she could hardly move. Across the street were three motels. She trudged over to what looked like the cheapest one, only to find it full. When she got the same response at the second one, panic once again started its little dance in her head. The third place did have a room, one for smokers, and it cost twice what she had budgeted for her first night on the road. She lay across the bed and fell asleep before she could enjoy a hot shower or cable television.

*T*he alignment was easy to fix; what she didn't plan on was the news that her brakes were shot. According to the stout, no-nonsense mechanic, she would be inviting grave danger by driving all the way to Atlanta without a new set of brakes.

By now the sun was high in a clear sky, setting the landscape alive with sparkles, and Jana had indulged in a breakfast of eggs, sausage, and pancakes. She'd stood in the shower a long time and tried not to think about how little progress she'd made toward Mom and Christmas. But she was ready to face whatever came, prepared to resume the long journey.

A new set of brakes, however, was not in her postcollege, prejob budget. Jana finally did what she most wanted not to do: called Dad. He and Barbra arrived a couple hours later in their four-wheel-drive pickup. Dad talked to the mechanic, told him to do what needed to be done, and then they took Jana back to Colorado Springs.

She heard Dad talking on the phone awhile later and figured out that Mom was on the other end. Of course they were talking about Jana—it was the only reason they talked anymore. Jana turned up the television, uncomfortable hearing herself referred to in the third person. When Dad came into the living room, she already knew what he was going to say.

"Mom doesn't want you driving all that way alone. Weather's bad all across the Midwest. So we'll get you on the first flight we can."

"Is she still on the line?"

"No, I think I woke her up."

Jana glanced at him. "Mom can't afford the airfare, and I can't either."

"I'll take care of it." Dad sounded weary.

"I'm sorry—I didn't know about the brakes. Haven't had any trouble at all."

"Oh, those things happen. Goes with having a car."

Barbra walked in. She was almost as slender as Jana, but her eyes had the look of someone who had been desperate many times. Jana had made a point of not learning Barbra's history, but she knew there was a previous marriage in it.

"It's probably a good thing you went off the road," Barbra said as she sat on the arm of the sofa, next to Dad. "Better to slide off the road now than have the brakes fail when you're going eighty down the interstate." Dad nodded, always in agreement with Barbra. Jana had thought this very thing herself but didn't say so.

*S*he stayed another two nights and felt even more guilty when Dad absorbed the seven-hundred-dollar expense of getting her a plane ticket to Atlanta this close to Christmas. But what could she do? Whether it was Beverly giving her a free meal or Dad financing her transportation needs, Jana was dependent on others' generosity. As Dad and

Barbra drove her to the airport early Thursday morning, she felt herself being carried through a life she didn't want but couldn't change.

"I don't want to make this trip," she said suddenly from the backseat of the Nissan. Barbra's head swiveled around in surprise.

"You don't?"

"Oh, it'll be warmer in Atlanta," Dad said, not taking his eyes from the road.

"Don, that's not what she means." Barbra turned to face Jana, eager to be helpful. "You don't want to see your mom like that, do you?"

Jana shrugged, angry at herself for bringing this up. "I hardly know these people."

"You don't know Aunt Cheryl?" Dad glanced at her in the rearview mirror.

"It's not that. They live in a whole other world. I just don't feel like dealing with unfamiliar surroundings."

"But it's in your grandparents' house—we've taken you there since you were a baby."

"That's not what I mean, Dad."

"Oh." He seemed to think about that. "What do you mean?"

Jana shook her head, not sure what she meant. "Forget it. I'm just tired of traveling, I guess."

While she sat in the airport, she watched a young woman wrestle a toddler and an infant. Besides her diaper bag she was hauling a small suitcase on wheels and a large shopping bag, unwrapped presents peeking out of it. The toddler was trying to run away while Mom attempted to discreetly nurse the baby. Mom looked frustrated beyond endurance. Jana was about to move closer and offer to help when a guy came over, carrying fast food, a backpack strapped on—apparently the husband and father. He caught Jana staring at the toddler and grinned.

"He'll crash any minute—hasn't slept since four this morning."

Mom chimed in. "Our flight last night was canceled."

"Oh my gosh—you spent the night here?" They smiled, and Jana marveled at their good humor.

"All so that Grandma and Grandpa can see the babies," the woman said. "I think next time we'll pay to have them fly to us."

Dad pulled the toddler back from charging someone's luggage cart, and the child had a meltdown, his shrieks raising looks from three different gates. Jana silently promised herself never to travel with children.

In fact, maybe she just wouldn't travel for a while. She and her little car had gone to college, to summer jobs, in and out of three different apartments with one set of college roommates and two different boyfriends. After the divorce, she and Mom had moved from the western suburbs to a smaller condo in a city neighborhood. She'd done nothing but pack and unpack for about six years.

I keep going places, but I don't seem to get anywhere. She pondered this as she boarded the plane, stuffed her carry-on in the overhead compartment, and edged into the last available middle seat. *Why is that? Why doesn't anyplace feel like home anymore?*

She did her best to relax without leaning into the people on either side of her. She concentrated on her physical existence—where her feet were, how her neck felt—because if she faced her emotional state she would have to cry for a very long time. She would never feel completely at home with Dad again. Too much had happened. She would always love him, but she found it hard to enjoy him and almost impossible to trust him. Deep down, she hoped he would make it with Barbra. Barbra seemed like a nice person, a woman who didn't deserve to be dumped the way Mom had been dumped. It would be refreshing to see real stability in Dad for a change. But Jana could not depend on him, and suddenly that made her so sad that she opened the in-flight catalogue and worked through it page by page, reading all the descriptions of luggage and travel gadgets and hundreds of items that most people would never figure out they needed.

She tried not to imagine what Mom looked like. She didn't

want to know how her color was or whether she had hair or if she was in a lot of pain. Mom would probably not die, but it was impossible to know for sure. So Jana must prepare to be the anchor for her own life. She was only twenty-two, but she must be older now. She must be the foundation for herself. She tried to imagine what life she would create by the time she was thirty, but that only made her stomach knot.

As the plane dipped to one side and circled Atlanta in preparation to land, the patches of green trees and yellow parks far below looked welcoming compared to the barrenness and whiteness of the north. When Jana took a taxi to her Aunt Cheryl's neighborhood, the air was chilly and damp—the drippy, greenish kind of moisture that smelled like very old backyards and very old houses with big porches.

Aunt Cheryl had lived in Grandma and Grandpa Murray's house since before both of them passed away. She'd been married briefly more than thirty years ago, but her husband was killed in Vietnam, leaving her with no children. She had been young enough to marry again and have children with someone else, but she chose Jesus instead and had been fully involved with the First Baptist Church ever since. Jana recalled hearing Aunt Cheryl say, years ago, at some family gathering, "I've had a very full life. I have no regrets." She said it with the resolve of a soldier—or a Southern woman of iron—the proverbial steel magnolia. Jana was not convinced that being at church three or four times a week would make anyone's life full in a healthy way. But she had no reason to argue with Aunt Cheryl, who'd never done anything but good for her and Mom. Aunt Cheryl was ten years older than Mom and had served as a sort of mother during the twelve or more years that Grandma had been gone.

Aunt Cheryl wore pastel pantsuits, and her face was always tastefully made up. She was slender and orderly, and Jana figured that this orderly pleasantness was why Mom had decided to live here for a while. The chemo had worn her out; she was on leave from her job. She needed to be somewhere that was under someone else's control. Aunt Cheryl seemed to be really good at control, the main reason Jana had always felt nervous around her.

The taxi took her past a huge red brick church with columns, and Jana recognized it as Aunt Cheryl's church. Southern Baptist, rather well-to-do. It had both a baby grand piano and a pipe organ. The choir members wore burgundy and gold robes. It was all coming back to Jana now. She'd never liked church; she thought it was because Dad always said church was where losers went to find the camaraderie of other losers. Now that she was older, Jana didn't know if Dad really meant it or if he just talked that way to irritate Mom. But the loser image had stuck with Jana, and every time she was in Atlanta and visited church with Aunt Cheryl, she felt that she had compromised something.

I'll go for Mom's sake. Mom's life now consisted of prayer and hope and searching for faith. Her letters contained references to church and church people. Although Mom hadn't been a churchgoer all the years Jana was growing up, Jana was pretty sure she had never really stopped believing all the Jesus stuff. Not that many weeks ago, back in their Chicago apartment, Jana overheard Mom praying, and it sounded like a prayer that some television evangelist would pray, full of phrases built around Jesus' name. Since the cancer came, Jana had prayed some, privately, figuring it wouldn't hurt. But she couldn't quite bring herself to pray the way she heard Mom pray that evening, locked in her room.

Jana prayed now, sort of, as she got out of the car and the driver pulled her luggage from the trunk. She saw Aunt Cheryl appear at the door, her face in the center of a huge holly wreath that hung over the window. Jana said, low enough that the taxi driver couldn't hear, "God, help me do this. I'm not even asking for a nice Christmas—I'm making this trip because of family obligations. Just help me be a good daughter while I'm here."

Aunt Cheryl's voice was lilty, and her hug was bony. She smelled of something light and floral, and her delicately structured face had acquired some lines around her mouth and eyes. The light brown hair was in place, in the same style it had held for decades.

"Sweetheart, I'm so glad you made it. Sorry about your *car.*" Her accent tended to put a strange emphasis on the last word of a sentence, something Jana had forgotten until just now.

"Well, it's an old car, and it's taken me a lot of places." She walked into the high-ceilinged sitting room and felt the weight of drapes and matching wallpaper, of heavy furniture and knickknacks with all sorts of family meanings behind them.

"Jana? I'm in here." Mom's voice was fairly strong. Jana followed the sound, turned a corner, and entered the small family room. Mom was sitting in an olive green recliner that faced the television. She wore a periwinkle blue robe and matching slippers that looked bright against her washed-out skin. Her face was puffy, and she still had a little hair. Her eyes looked good, though, and her smile made Jana's throat ache. She hugged her mother, trying not to sit on top of her.

"Sorry I didn't get up. Had radiation this morning. So I'm pretty worthless for a while."

Jana sat in a chair nearby and wiped her eyes.

"How was your flight?"

"Fine."

"I didn't like the idea of your driving all that way by yourself anyway."

Jana noticed that Mom's Southern accent had returned just

a bit. There was a slight change in her vowels and some upward inflection that usually wasn't there. It was kind of charming.

"Was your visit with Dad okay?" Mom never mentioned Barbra.

"Sure. You know Dad. He makes everything an event."

Aunt Cheryl laughed politely from the sofa. Mom just smiled. "Well, I know it means a lot to him that you went for a visit."

Even though it was two in the afternoon, Aunt Cheryl had prepared lunch—chicken pasta soup and grilled-cheese sandwiches. She made a pot of cinnamon tea and brought out Christmas cookies for dessert.

After they ate and visited awhile, Mom excused herself to nap in her bedroom, which was Grandma's old room on the first floor. Aunt Cheryl carried Jana's suitcase upstairs for her.

"We'll put you in my old bedroom, closest to the bathroom."

"Where will you sleep?"

"Oh, my room is next to the stairs. Most of the time now I sleep in the family room, so I can hear your mom if she needs anything."

Jana's room was wallpapered with delicate vertical stripes in colors that reminded her of the plastic dishes they used to take on picnics. She had to move figurines aside in order to place her overnight bag on the dresser. A painting of a girl and a horse in a lush pasture hung directly above the walnut bed. She sat on the bed for a moment and silently observed that she had just entered another universe, one crowded with other people's memories and loves. She longed to go sit with her mother. She longed to go back to Chicago right now.

She wandered around upstairs, getting reacquainted with her mother's family. Their photos formed a large gallery along the wall in the hallway. She recognized Grandma and Grandpa Murray's wedding picture, Mom's and Aunt Cheryl's baby pictures, a great-uncle and his family, two great-aunts and theirs. There was a faded aerial shot of the farm Grandpa's brother owned until he died. There was Grandma's sister and her husband, dressed up in Easter colors, standing in front of a new Buick. None of the pictures were taken any later than the 1970s, as far as Jana could tell.

Jana remembered Grandma and Grandpa from early childhood. They could have walked right out of Norman Rockwell paintings; Grandma always wore an apron, and Grandpa smoked cigars. Jana remembered the scent of them, Grandma sweet like cookie dough, and Grandpa pungent with tobacco and soap. She remembered their smiles and their eyes scrunched happily behind heavy-framed glasses. They were both gone before Jana reached her teens.

At the end of the hallway, near the door of the bedroom Jana occupied, was a picture of Uncle Jackson, Aunt Cheryl's husband, in a dress uniform. Jana had never met him; she was born ten years after his helicopter went down behind enemy lines. There was a wedding picture of Jackson and Aunt Cheryl. She didn't look much like the person she was now. She was just a kid, barely out of high school. Her smile was open and devoid of real experience. Underneath Jackson's air force photo was a framed funeral notice and obituary. Jana read it, as she had on every visit here. This time, though, it felt ominous. The brief history of Jackson's whole life seemed an insult. Surely he was more than a person who had graduated from this high school and belonged to that community organization. The summary said nothing about who he really was, except "devoted husband and son." He was survived by "his wife, Cherylynn Murray Hodge." Jana realized then that young Cherylynn looked a lot like Mom had years ago, when Jana was little. They had the same smile, the same narrow chin. But now, in both women, fine lines and sorrowful years had taken over, as if a person's life was nothing more than a long walk toward death.

Jana escaped the hallway of faces and glanced at her own in the mirror above the bedroom dresser. She had Dad's chin but Mom's eyes. What did it matter? She would die too. In fact, she felt tired enough to do that right now. She was glad for the quiet, a large, soft bed, and a door that would shut.

*S*he didn't expect to sleep so much in her grandparents' house. Especially with Mom sick right downstairs, she thought she would lie awake, listening for sounds of discomfort. But instead she slept and slept. The bed was soft and springy, and she was surrounded by comforters and afghans and small pillows in those plastic colors. Aunt Cheryl kept appearing at the door, quiet and smiley. Jana came downstairs for meals, and she tried to sit in the warm family room and talk with Mom, but everything took so much effort.

Before she knew it, four days had gone by, and she'd hardly left the house. All she wanted to do was sleep. She dragged herself down to breakfast Monday morning. Mom and Aunt Cheryl looked at her intently.

"Jana," Mom said, "have you been sleeping like this at home?"

Home? Which home do you mean? "No. I usually don't sleep much. Maybe I have the flu."

"I've never seen you lethargic like this. I want you to go to the doctor. Aunt Cheryl can make an appointment for you at her internist's."

"No, Mom, I don't need a doctor."

"I'm worried. You've not been like this before, at least not when you've been around me. Just go for a blood test, a simple physical. They can check for anemia or mono or something."

Because the last thing she wanted to do was create more stress for Mom, she made the appointment. Aunt Cheryl managed to get her to the doctor that afternoon. Jana acquiesced to having a thorough examination, to having blood drawn from her arm, to giving a sample of her urine. They would have results in a couple of days.

"Well, at least he didn't see anything apparently wrong," Aunt Cheryl commented as they drove toward home. "He didn't look at you and pronounce something."

"Do they ever do that?" Jana was only mildly curious.

"Sometimes. My cousin had a thyroid condition, and the doctor guessed it the minute she walked in. Something about her eyes protruding."

"Yuck."

"I'm stopping to pick up a few things. Any favorite foods you want?" Aunt Cheryl was guiding the car into the parking lot of Kroger.

A huge bottle of Merlot, enough to get me through New Year's. "Do we have eggnog?" Jana knew that Aunt Cheryl had not a drop of alcohol in the house, but a person could drink eggnog and pretend it was spiked.

"It's already on my list." Aunt Cheryl smiled. "It's just not Christmas without eggnog."

They shopped quickly because Aunt Cheryl had a list, and

Jana was in no mood to browse. She just wanted to go home and rest some more.

They were only a few blocks from the house when Jana worked up the nerve to ask her aunt the question she had been pushing back since she arrived.

"How do you think Mom is doing?"

"The specialist gives her good reports. She's responded to the chemo real well."

Jana thought the response too quick. "But what do *you* think? You're the one who's with her all the time. And you know her better than anybody."

Aunt Cheryl pressed her lips together. Sunglasses hid her eyes. "This is a bigger struggle than the cancer. I think that, physically, she can beat it. But it's a hard time in your mother's life."

"The divorce didn't help."

"Yes, divorce brings its own form of devastation. There are other things too."

They had pulled into the drive, and Aunt Cheryl turned off the engine. They sat, the large house with its brick face and dark green shutters towering over them. Aunt Cheryl took off her sunglasses and shifted in the seat to look at Jana.

"I think your mom lost herself for a while, you know, in a spiritual way. Your dad always discouraged any sort of religious life, but Della had grown up with it. She had to trade it for marriage, I think."

"I don't think Mom would sell out like that." Jana noticed a sudden, bitter taste, usually a sign that she was angry. Of course Aunt Cheryl would turn all of this into something spiritual.

"Oh, that's not what I mean. She left her faith on her own, like a lot of people did back in the sixties and seventies. Your mom was always the creative sort, and she had to try things out. But now..." Aunt Cheryl looked away, seeming to search. "I think that most people, sooner or later, have to at least face their parents' faith and wrestle with it. And sometimes they don't return to it, but other times they do. Della's trying to understand what she needs to do."

Jana looked out at the magnolia tree that shaded the drive-way. She decided not to mention hearing Mom pray back in Chicago. She felt so tired, and there was too much in her life to process right now. "So you think this spiritual struggle might affect Mom's getting over the cancer?"

"Oh, I don't know." Aunt Cheryl studied her car keys. "We're not just bodies. We're souls, too. All of it works together."

"Thanks for taking care of Mom." Jana's voice failed her suddenly. Before she knew it, both she and Aunt Cheryl were crying. They didn't touch or even look at each other, just gasped in the silence of the closed car. Aunt Cheryl got a box of tissues from the glove compartment, and they blew their noses.

"I'm just so grateful I can do this, sweetheart. It's an honor to care for people you love. We all cared for Daddy, here in this house, until he died. I hated that Mother died in the hospital, but she went fast." Aunt Cheryl looked at Jana again, her delicate face moist around the eyes, her makeup smudged. "I truly believe your mom is going to survive. I think she's about to start a whole other life." She grasped Jana's hand. "And you have no idea what it means to her that you're here, Mary Georgianna. You're the pride of her life, you know."

They carried in groceries. Jana watched Aunt Cheryl move quickly up the back steps and wondered how a woman with so much sorrow could walk so lightly.

THE
ENCOUNTER

*C*hurch on Sunday was something to be endured, nothing more. Jana just wanted to close her eyes and not hear so many hymns. And because it was the holiday season, of course the service was longer and had all sorts of special features. Some woman with gray hair who was wearing about five scarves performed a dramatic reading; she was supposed to be the mother of John the Baptist. Jana couldn't picture women back then wearing lavender lipstick.

Jesus' name was everywhere. They used phrases such as "lordship" and "traveling mercies." (A lot of people in the congregation were traveling over the holidays, so they needed special mercy from God, designed just for the road?) Jana's head was spinning, but mainly it was tired. The church was overheated and stuffy, and people were way too friendly, considering they hardly knew her.

After the service Aunt Cheryl introduced Jana to yet another woman "who's a dear friend." Her name was Sandra, and Jana was relieved to see before her a person she might actually like to talk to. The woman wore little makeup and smiled but not too much, which gave her a welcoming presence.

"Cheryl and Della are really glad you're here," Sandra said. "It's good to be with family at holiday time." Jana heard herself piping out this trite statement. It was the best she could do, but she hated the sound of it.

"Cheryl tells me you've been pretty fatigued."

Of course. No secrets around here. "I think all the traveling caught up with me."

"It's emotionally tiring, too—going from one parent to another, seeing your mother sick." Sandra took a drink of coffee and nodded to someone behind Jana. Jana looked at her, not knowing how to respond. She hadn't expected anything so direct, or so true.

"Well, everybody has to adjust," she said. "Maybe I just picked up a bug."

"Have you ruled out low thyroid?"

"I went to the doctor day before yesterday. They sucked out some bodily fluids and are supposed to call in a day or so."

Sandra laughed, which gave Jana further indication that she was in safe company. Most people in this crowd would not appreciate *any* mention of bodily fluids. She allowed herself to laugh too.

"You remind me of my daughter—that droll sense of humor." Sandra's eyes were dove gray, her ash blond hair cut in a layered bob that required no accessories. She looked soft and strong at the same time. And she was studying Jana but in a way that didn't feel threatening.

"If you're sleeping a lot for no clear reason," she said, "you might be depressed."

"You sound like a therapist."

Sandra gave a little smile. "Have you been to a therapist?"

"For a while, back at school." *Divorce brings its own form of devastation.* "It's like a rite of passage, I guess."

"College years are full of transition, and that's usually when people need support. And you're partially right. I do spiritual direction, which is a type of therapy, I suppose."

Jana nodded but had no reply.

"I live just a few streets over from your aunt's. Would you like to come see me?"

"I'm really not looking for spiritual direction." Jana hoped she didn't sound hostile, but her first impulse was self-defense, especially lately, when there seemed to be so little of her life left to defend.

"Oh, it's not as intimidating as it sounds. I just listen and help people figure out what they already know."

Jana sensed a strange pull from those soft eyes, but she had to fight just a little. "You guys set me up, didn't you?"

"Cheryl's a good friend of mine. She just mentioned your symptoms. It's not a conspiracy."

As the crowd moved around them and all the voices swirled into deafening noise, the thought of escaping Aunt

Cheryl's home and Mom's illness for even an hour was suddenly appealing. Jana imagined that wherever this woman lived must be quiet and uncluttered. "Are you sure you want company so close to Christmas?"

Sandra made a dismissive motion with her hand. "I'm not traveling, and my kids are coming in a couple of days. You can catch me between batches of peanut brittle."

The next day, while Aunt Cheryl was making divinity and fudge and Mom was decorating cookies—both giggling like little girls at the wide kitchen table—Jana put on her jacket and walked three blocks south and four blocks east. For the first time—possibly because this was her first real walk since arriving here—she noticed that all the trees were about twice as tall as those in Chicago. They were gigantic, bending over shady sidewalks and ivy-covered yards. Jana felt as if she were being watched every step of the way. Sandra's house was large, dark brick, with two pine trees guarding the house. A narrow walk curved up to the front door.

Sandra answered the doorbell quickly. She wore not an apron but a turtleneck and jeans. She showed Jana to a small office down the hall and away from the main rooms of the house.

"Coffee, tea, soda?" Sandra put a plate of Christmas cookies on the small coffee table between them. Jana declined both food and drink. She sat on a love seat facing Sandra, who pulled up what looked like an antique dining room chair. The window to Sandra's left was filled with potted plants, giving an appealing green tint to the light coming in. The room itself was small and—as Jana had expected—quiet; it faced the back of the property, sheltered from any street sounds. The walls, draperies, and furniture were understated, but Jana had an overall sense of the color cinnamon around her.

Once she sat down, she realized that she had come without any plan, with no idea of what to talk about. Her discomfort increased when it became clear that Sandra had no agenda either. They sat in silence an interminable few moments, while Jana's thoughts jumbled into a random order of importance. She grabbed an idea and started talking.

"I'm not sure how to help my mom right now."

This was a good move, and they spent the next twenty minutes talking through cancer treatment and all that went with it. Sandra hit on the questions that helped Jana organize both fear and sorrow so that she could look at them more clearly.

But as the afternoon light shifted and sent a tangerine hue across the room, Sandra leaned back in her chair and delivered a sentence that threw the rest of their conversation onto another track entirely.

"Jana, I have the feeling that there's a huge question you're afraid to ask."

"What's that?"

"You tell me."

Well, this *was* therapy, after all. Jana shrugged and looked at the window plants.

"When you flew into town, what was the one thing that concerned you most?"

"How to deal with all this—like what we've been talking about." She dared to look at Sandra again and encountered an expression completely calm and without judgment. Other thoughts began to form then, and she decided to just say whatever came to mind.

"I know that Mom's faith is really important to her right now. But it's not my faith, and I don't know what I'm supposed to do."

Sandra said nothing and seemed to be waiting.

"But I feel like I need to be supportive—go to church and all that—because Mom needs it. When I was growing up we never even went to church, so all this is new to me."

"What do you think of your mom's faith?"

"It's all right, I guess. It's something she needs. And, well, it's Christmas, so I shouldn't feel so weird about Christianity."

She reached finally for a cookie and changed her position on the love seat. "Maybe I should at least try to understand what she believes. That shouldn't be so hard. I mean, Aunt Cheryl would be glad to explain it, but I know if I ask one question, she'll take that as a signal to convert me, and I'm not interested in converting."

"No, I don't think you need another person telling you about Christianity."

"Maybe I should try to pray with Mom. I could offer to pray with her before bed or something."

Sandra's high, smooth forehead was shadowed by a few strands of hair. "Do you *want* to pray?"

"I don't know. I probably should. But I don't."

"How do you process what's going on inside you?"

Jana had to think. "I've kept a journal for a while."

Sandra's eyes flashed a little. "That's a great way to work things out. And if you pray at all, you're probably doing it through your writing."

Jana took a bite of the cookie. Ginger and orange. She examined the treat rather than engage Sandra's gaze again. She had entered this conversation willingly but felt exposed now. She never talked to people about her journals, not even friends.

"I think you could use your journal writing to get to know your mom's faith. To work through some of the questions you've been afraid to ask." Sandra got up and took a book from the shelf on the far wall. Jana could see that it was a Bible.

"There's a writing exercise you can do. And given that we're just a few days from Christmas, this could be a perfect fit."

She sat next to Jana and paged through the Bible until she

came to Luke's gospel. She pointed to a verse in the middle of the first chapter. "The actual Christmas story that everyone knows begins in chapter 2, but Mary's story begins here."

"Oh, I know that," Jana said quickly. "Everybody knows about Mary and Joseph and the baby in the manger and all that."

"I'm suggesting that you explore this in a different way." Sandra positioned the ribbon bookmark on that page and closed the Bible. "I'm suggesting that you meet Mary—Mary in this story. Read the story in the Bible, and then close the book and write the story yourself."

"Rewrite the Bible?"

"What you do is simply enter the story. Enter the story and walk beside Mary, and talk to her. Ask her any questions you like."

Jana regarded the Bible but didn't reach for it.

"This exercise is based on a spiritual tradition that goes back centuries. You are merely engaging your imagination with the story. Now, as a Christian, I believe that God meets you in that story and tells you what you need to understand. But it's something you enter freely and willingly, and there's no other person hanging around putting pressure on you. And I can tell you from my own experience"—she smiled—"that God is gentle with us and will take you only as far as you're able and willing to go."

Jana looked at the book in Sandra's hands. It could pass for some hardcover novel—not an important looking leatherbound edition, at least. "It could be interesting."

"It could. Just an idea. Do you want to borrow this?"

"I'm sure we've got Bibles over at Aunt Cheryl's."

Sandra seemed to know that she'd gone far enough. She placed the Bible on the coffee table and rose from the love seat. Jana got up too, relieved this was over. But she did like the room. She took a last glance toward the window full of plants as they walked into the hallway.

"So," she said, "is this something you would read later?"

"No, I don't plan to read any of it. But I'd be happy to talk with you once you've done it." They came to the front door. "I'm glad you stopped by. Don't be shy to come again, okay?"

"What do I owe you?"

"Nothing. Merry Christmas." As Jana walked out the door, Sandra touched her lightly on the shoulder.

The day outside felt way too warm for December 22. Her surroundings felt precisely un-Christmasy. She walked in and out of patches of sunlight and considered the proposed writing assignment. Then she remembered the one or two teachers back in junior high and high school who had the nerve to give assignments to be done during the holiday break. Well, here she was again, feeling both dutiful and irritated.

She'd kept journals since she was eleven or so. She couldn't stand to go back and read them now, but she couldn't bear to throw them away either. They were parts of herself that were not only important but completely embarrassing.

"I'm an adult now, "she announced to the oak tree that leaned over the street. She was winding down a hill, well-kept houses on both sides, their yards looking either overgrown with planned ground cover or shaved down to nearly bare ground. Shrubs everywhere. Damper than Chicago. Darker somehow, maybe because everything here felt so old. The houses might be new, but still they looked old. They made Jana think of families that were still together, of grandmas placing large trays of golden brown turkey on long oval tables, of greenery and candles planted on ledges and hung in windows.

"I'm an adult now, and I don't have to do anything I don't want to do. I don't even know this woman. And in a few days I'll be back in Chicago."

She murmured all of this as shrubbery and quiet, stately windows watched her passing.

*A*unt Cheryl and Mom had company that evening, two elderly women from church. Myrtle had never married and had no children to visit her on holidays. Angie had children, but they were grown, and only one would be able to make it to Atlanta this year. The four women chattered and laughed around the dining room table, plates piled with stuffed Cornish hens and cranberry salad and sweet potato soufflé. Jana listened in mild detachment as Myrtle and Angie recounted the events of their week. It seemed that they derived a lot of excitement from what would be mundane events to most people. There was the Adventure of the Wrong Can of Cranberries, set at the local supermarket. The villain was a young girl stocking shelves who didn't know the difference between cranberry sauce that was smooth and sauce that had whole cranberries in it.

"Who would think that a person who works in a grocery would not be familiar with cranberries?" Angie said this with a dramatic wave of her hand. It was liver-spotted and heavily veined. She wore diamond and gold bands on the middle and ring fingers.

There was the Saga of the Brother-in-Law in Shreveport who might lose his house because a home-improvement company had convinced him to borrow against the house in order to fix it. "What these people do is get you in hock up to your eyebrows buying home improvement, and then when you can't make your payments, they take your house. Imagine!" Myrtle was unassuming in every other way, but her deep voice boomed across the crystal and china.

Mom and Aunt Cheryl appeared delighted and relaxed; obviously they'd been friends of these women for some time.

Jana was able to sit back too, relieved of any responsibility for making the evening go well. And although she couldn't get excited about cranberry varieties, she felt some affection toward Myrtle and Angie. For one thing, they didn't appear obligated to ask Jana questions about herself. She was included but not put upon to join the conversation. She had the feeling that— maybe because of their age—the two visitors no longer concerned themselves with other people's trivia. They were beyond having to impress anyone, and they said what they thought. She liked that.

They had an early dinner, so the dishes were done and the guests gone by eight. Mom was clearly fatigued from the evening, and she settled into bed. Aunt Cheryl was making snowball cookies and two kinds of bread, a CD of Christmas hand-bell music chiming melodies from the top of the refrigerator. She appeared totally absorbed, and Jana decided not to offer help.

She did ask to borrow the car and then asked for directions to the nearest bookstore or card shop. As she got in the car, she noticed that it was chillier than during the afternoon, finally weather that felt something like the Christmases to which Jana was accustomed. She followed the directions written on a slip of paper in her lap. The journey brought her to a mid-size shopping mall, its parking lot full at nearly nine in the evening. Jana walked in the entrance and immediately sensed the shoppers' anxiety and too many aromas in the air and a complete excess of decoration. She wished that Christmas could just be skipped every few years, starting with this one. What a holiday that would be.

But the bookstore proved as seductive as bookstores always were. She opened covers and scanned pages, feeling thirsty for words. She hadn't known desire like this in weeks; the holidays had deadened everything in her. Hurrying past the Christmas fluff and loud displays, she looked at biographies and histories, at new fiction and poetry.

She found a rack of journals and wanted to buy at least four of them. Cloth covers were her favorites because of the texture, but sometimes the better art was on the smooth, padded ones. She bought two, one just because she loved the way it looked, the other because she was actually considering writing this Mary thing that Sandra had suggested. It looked as if the several days ahead of her were each going to end with Mom's going to bed early and Aunt Cheryl's being preoccupied with her Christmas rituals. The activities left to Jana would be watching television or writing. Television was full of holiday nostalgia and advertising. Jana was suddenly grateful for the writing assignment. She realized that she hadn't written much in nearly two months, for one reason or another—travel, dealing with Dad's life, missing Gary, dealing with Mom's life. Sometimes her emotions had all they could manage just getting through the day. But with a new journal in hand she might get lost in writing again. It could turn out to be her real buffer against everything else.

She passed a life-size nativity scene on the way out of the mall. The Mary figure looked like some fragile yet exquisite European actress—fine features, ivory skin, narrow, pretty eyes.

Mary was a Jewish girl, right? Well, scrap this model. At the very least, the actual Mary would have been Semitic, with darker complexion and hair. A person came to mind then, from her sophomore year: Jeanine Arnold, whose mother was Jewish in the fullest sense of the word, by faith as well as ethnicity, and had grown up in Tel Aviv. Jeanine had come to the U.S. as a child. Her father was American and not particularly religious. (Jana wondered if men in general just didn't have that religion gene, since in so many cases the women carried on that part of life, as Jeanine's mother had and as Mom might have.) Jeanine wasn't movie-star beautiful, but she had distinctive features: intense eyes, thick dark hair, light olive skin, and a body that was full but not really overweight. Jeanine had presence without being pretentious. She was probably much closer to the image of Mary in the Bible than all those breakable nativity clones.

Jana was in the car now, pulling out of the glutted parking lot, trying to read the directions, only now in reverse, to get her back to Aunt Cheryl's. "She could look a little like Jeanine, and

I'll make her nineteen. Back then girls probably married a lot earlier, but this is my story, right? I can do whatever I want." She could turn it into a farce, like a skit on *Saturday Night Live*. She remembered SNL reruns of early shows with Gilda Radner—now *she* would be the Mary of all Marys. Wild hair and dorky glasses, belly out to here, arguing with the manager of the Motel 6: "You think *I* want to have this baby—I didn't even have *sex* to get this baby. *God* put it in me. I wasn't real hot on the idea, but, you know, a good Jewish girl doesn't argue with *God*. So why should I sleep out on the street? You've got a nice futon in there. You don't rent out your apartment? How could you even think of charging *God* rent anyway? What are you, sacrilegious?" Jana pulled into Aunt Cheryl's drive and realized that she was smiling broadly in the darkness.

Every evening she went to her mother's room to sit for a while. Mom talked about the past, which seemed really inappropriate, given that Mom was only forty-eight. Eighty-year-old people talked about the past. Jana wondered if Mom believed she would die from this cancer. There was no reason to assume that right now; she was responding well to the therapy even though the cure made her sick and tired.

But Mom talked about her mother and father.

"Being in this house brings up a lot of memories," she said that night when Jana sat in the easy chair next to the bed. "It's amazing how an object, like the salt-and-pepper shakers on the table tonight, can bring back so much. Your grandfather collected salt-and-pepper shakers. Did you know that?"

Jana shook her head.

"I think he had about forty sets before he died. Cousin Gladys claimed most of them, said that Dad had promised them to her son, Charles."

"Did you believe her?"

"Oh." Mom fingered the quilt, one that some grandma or aunt had stitched decades before. "Gladys was always kind of grabby. She collected *stuff*. Didn't throw things away. Thought it would all come in handy—or be worth a fortune someday. We'd been through so much when Dad was sick, and once he was gone, none of us had the energy to argue with Gladys. Wish I'd saved a couple of sets for you though."

Jana offered a light laugh. "They would be wasted on me, Mom. I don't even cook."

"I know." Mom looked sad. "I didn't pass on much to you, did I?"

"You passed on all the important things—intelligence and good looks." Jana smiled big, hoping to force that sadness from her mother.

"It takes more than that. I didn't realize it until the past few months. You need history, too. You need something older than you that you can hold on to when your own abilities fail."

Jana didn't know what to say. In this house she was surrounded by history, but most of it was unintelligible to her. She had come here once a year during most of her childhood, but the hours then were taken up with playing in the deep shade of the backyard and shopping in the afternoons with Mom and Grandma and sometimes Aunt Cheryl. Jana remembered playing with kids in the neighborhood. She remembered dressing up in clothes from the closet in the study upstairs.

"Cheryl's gathered a whole shoebox of old photos, and we're sorting through them. We'll have them restored and make copies, and you and I can take some back to Chicago with us."

This was a good sign, talking about Chicago.

"Do you want me to take you to treatment tomorrow, Mom?"

"Sure. It would be nice to give Cheryl a break."

She kissed Mom good night and went upstairs to her room. After washing her face and putting on pajamas, she padded downstairs to make herself a cup of cocoa. She took a short detour into the sitting room and said good night to Aunt Cheryl before returning to her room and shutting the door, grateful for the solitude.

She wondered if she should at least locate a Bible, in case she decided to try the writing exercise. She slipped down the hall to the far west room, the little study. It still had the old desk and hideaway bed. The wall behind the desk was one continuous built-in bookcase. Jana scanned the titles. There were a lot of gardening books, some old novels, a set of encyclopedias printed in 1978, and one entire section of Bible study booklets, probably used at Aunt Cheryl's church. At the end of that shelf was a study Bible still in its box. She took it and noticed that several heavy reference books leaned against one another on the shelf below. One title read *Encyclopedia of Bible Lands and Customs.* She pulled it out and flipped through pages, finding pictures of holy sites, Middle Eastern plants and animals, and chapters on family life, social customs, and pivotal events.

This and the Bible she took with her back to bed. She couldn't bring herself to read the Bible story yet, and she was not inspired to write. So she ended up reading the encyclopedia for an hour. By that time a young woman with dark hair was standing at some doorway in Jana's mind. She was taking form, gathering an environment around her. Jana settled back against the pillows and closed her eyes. Burning on the insides of her eyelids were images from the book— arid valleys and olive groves, women in long dresses, and men selling spices, vegetables, and fabrics out of stalls in a village market.

It was nearly eleven when she picked up the Bible and read from the first chapter of Luke.

In the sixth month of Elizabeth's pregnancy, God sent the angel Gabriel to Nazareth, a village in Galilee, to a virgin named Mary. She was engaged to be married to a man named Joseph, a descendant of King David. Gabriel appeared to her and said, "Greetings, favored woman! The Lord is with you!"

Confused and disturbed, Mary tried to think what the angel could mean. "Don't be frightened, Mary," the angel told her, "for God has decided to bless you! You will become pregnant and have a son, and you are to name him Jesus. He will be very great and will be called the Son of the Most High. And the Lord God will give him the throne of his ancestor David. And he will reign over Israel forever; his Kingdom will never end!"

Mary asked the angel, "But how can I have a baby? I am a virgin."

The angel replied, "The Holy Spirit will come upon you, and the power of the Most High will overshadow you. So the baby born to you will be holy, and he will be called the Son of God. What's more, your relative Elizabeth has become pregnant in her old age! People used to say she was barren, but she's already in her sixth month. For nothing is impossible with God."

Mary responded, "I am the Lord's servant, and I am willing to accept whatever he wants. May everything you have said come true." And then the angel left.

I can't do this. Jana put down the Bible and tapped the pen against the blank journal. *Where do you begin? It's all miracles and things that don't even make sense.*

Sandra said that all she had to do was walk beside Mary. She could ask her questions if she wanted.

I'm in a small room in a stone house. It is late evening, and the light coming in the window is soft and gray-pink. It's very quiet.

She stands at the window, looking out at a vineyard that belongs to her parents. She looks like a person who is content with her life but who still has dreams of what other lives might be like.

Now I see that her expression is suddenly fearful. She is gazing to her right toward a corner of the room. I don't see anything. I come closer. "Are you all right?"

Her lips are moving, and she is trembling. The room remains quiet, but there is a strange charge to the air.

"I am the Lord's servant, and I am willing to accept whatever he wants. May everything you have said come true." She is still staring intently toward the corner. She's not trembling so much. She turns to the window again and resumes gazing at the vineyard. The only difference is that she is breathing faster now, as if she's been running.

I come closer and say very softly, "What happened?"

She looks at me, and I can see how young she is, how smooth her face is. "I can't really say."

"Please. I know something happened."

Her eyes are dark and calm. "You won't understand. You won't believe me." A look of worry crosses her features then. "No one will believe me. How can this ever come to be?"

"How can what come to be?" I touch her shoulder. She is warm and soft, like any young girl. She's just a person, after all.

She faces me then and measures me with her eyes. "Because you ask, I trust you will accept whatever I say."

"Yes, I will."

She takes my hand and draws me to sit on the floor beside her. She looks at me closely, to be sure I can be trusted, I suppose.

"Such a huge, bright creature. You didn't see him?"

"No. I couldn't see anything, but I could tell that you were looking at something."

"An angel. He was Gabriel—Gabriel who is named in sacred Scripture. My father has spoken of him."

I try to ignore the doubt in my mind about angels and other invisible beings. "What did Gabriel say?"

"God will make me pregnant, and my son will be a king."

We just look at each other. What can a person say to that?

"I've never heard of such a thing," I say.

"And my elderly cousin Elizabeth is six months pregnant."

"Elderly?"

"Yes." Mary looks at me as if I were a child who needs special help. "Much past the years of childbearing." Her eyes look beyond me, toward the ceiling, toward something in her own mind. "In our sacred writings there is a tradition of barren women made fertile in old age. The old women love to tell those stories."

"But you're not old. You're a virgin."

"Yes." She sighs then and looks toward the window. "What have I done?"

"You haven't done anything. It sounds as if something has happened to you."

"<u>Will</u> happen. It hasn't yet."

"How do you know?"

She shrugs. "I would know."

"I admire what you said, at the end."

"What?"

"About being the Lord's servant, being willing. This is huge—to take on, I mean."

"How could I say anything else?" A tear slips down her cheek. "I got up this morning, and I was just me, just my father's daughter engaged to be married to Joseph— Oh!"

Her hand flies to her face. "How can I tell Joseph? How can I tell anyone?" She rushes to the window and searches the sky. "Did Gabriel say anything about that and I forgot it? I have no idea what to do next." She turns to me, looking panicked. "What do I do next?"

For the first time I feel I have something useful to say to this girl. "You just do what you always do, the way you were doing before the angel came. If God is doing all of this to you, God must have a plan, don't you think?"

She slides down against the wall until she's sitting on the floor. "You're right. All I can do is wait." She looks up at me, seeming hopeful. "I am in God's plan. How did this happen?"

I have no answer to that.

The next morning Jana read what she'd written. It wasn't earthshaking, but she packed the journal in her bag when she took Mom for radiation treatment midmorning. She sat in the waiting room and felt slightly sickened by the smells of disinfectant and human suffering. Desperate not to look at anything around her, she pulled out the journal and wrote the first thing that came to mind.

A few days later I run into Mary at the well. We both have water jars to fill. We reach the well at the same moment, and our eyes meet. I can tell that it's happened.

"*Are you…?*" *I talk softly, not wanting to draw attention to us.*

"*Yes.*" *She smiles a strong smile.* "*The blood hasn't come, and the time is past for it. And…*" *She searches for words.* "*Early this morning I thought I was dreaming—the way you float in dreams. Do you know what I mean?*"

I nod.

"*And the room grew very warm, and I could feel something happening. There was power snapping inside me.*"

"*Were you scared?*"

"*No. There was so much joy. I think that is how a person feels when she is in the presence of God. I was so happy, so unafraid, so eager for my life to happen, so sure that everything would be fine.*" *She grasps my arm, her face bright.* "*Everything will be fine. You have to believe that.*"

I watch her walk away toward home, the jar balanced on her head. She is so young. That's all I can think about. She's young and doesn't know how hard everything can be. She is too young to fear the things that older people know about. Maybe this is why she was chosen. For this task, God needed a child.

As she waited for Mom, Jana wondered about Mary's mother. Did Mary tell her? Did she find any support there? What about her father? Back then didn't they stone women who turned up pregnant and unwed? Who could the girl even turn to? She mulled over all this until Mom appeared nearly two hours later. Jana saw the weary eyes and the brave smile, steeled herself, and helped Mom to the car. While driving back to the house, she tried to say all the right things, asking if she should turn up the heat, if they needed to stop at the pharmacy. Mom didn't need anything. She laughed a little when a mother and toddler crossed the road in front of them at a stoplight, the toddler little more than a bundle of bright pink parka, eyes and nose barely visible within the fur-rimmed hood. But Mom couldn't help but sigh a few times, a tired, pain-filled sigh—or maybe it was her attempt to get a deep breath. She smelled of medicine, of beds and too much sleep. When they got to Aunt Cheryl's, Mom changed into softer, lighter clothes and settled into the olive green recliner, TV remote in hand. One of the cable stations played classic movies, and Mom claimed she was catching up on films she'd missed years ago.

Aunt Cheryl had potato soup ready. Jana could barely taste it. She excused herself as soon as her bowl was empty and went upstairs. She changed clothes too, for no particular reason. Then she opened the Bible and read further into the Christmas story. She must get her mind somewhere else. Anywhere else.

She spent half an hour skimming the Holy Lands book. By then, she was itching just to write something, anything. If nothing else, she wanted to save the real Mary from the likes of the French-actress Mary in the gaudy shopping mall.

She put the pen on the cream-colored page, its lines fine and grayish, just visible enough to guide the pen.

I'm on the road to Bethlehem. I don't know how I got here or even who I am. But I know that I'm supposed to be here. At one crossroads I meet up with a caravan—maybe forty or fifty people. At the tail end of it, a girl about my age rides a donkey. She leans over the donkey's head as if she's in pain or very tired. She changes her position slightly, and I see that it's Mary, and she's pregnant—very pregnant. It looks as if she could have this baby any minute. A man several years older than she is guiding the donkey, taking care to lead it on the smoothest parts of the road. He must be Joseph.

Mary looks as if she's completely uncomfortable—and yet so patient with what's happening. I think that maybe pregnant women grow patient because they have to take time to grow and deliver babies. They have no choice but to wait. Mary looks as if she's waited a long time already.

I go up to the donkey and catch Mary's eye. I see that she recognizes me.

"I'm so glad you've come," she says.

"Are you all right?"

She closes her eyes for a moment—in pain, I think—and smiles when she opens them again to look at me.

"I'm all right. But my time is close. There's no way to get comfortable now."

"Wish I could do something for you."

"This is good." She smiles a little more. "Just talk to me. Keep me company and help me concentrate on something besides this." She glances down at the bulge underneath her clothes.

"I don't think I told you before, but we have the same name."

"Hello, Mary." She nods then toward the man. "This is my husband, Joseph." Hearing his name, Joseph looks back at us. He nods to me pleasantly but continues to concentrate on the road and the donkey.

"You're going to Bethlehem?" I ask her.

"Yes…for the census. You?"

I realize that I don't know where I'm going or why, but I answer, "I…have relatives in Bethlehem."

"My husband's family comes from Bethlehem, which is why we need to register there."

"Leave it to the Romans to make everything difficult."

She closes her eyes again. "Everything has a purpose, I guess."

"Have you been to Bethlehem before?"

"No. My husband and I have not been married very long. He has cousins there but hasn't visited for a couple of years." She leans toward me a little and speaks more softly. "I really don't want to make this trip—not now. I'm doing this because it's a family obligation. But it's the worst possible time, you know?"

Family obligations. Yes, I understand all about those.

"Everything will probably be fine," I say, sounding weak and stupid.

"Of course it will. I am in God's hands...and in God's will." Suddenly she looks older than she is. She seems very serious, too, and I hope I haven't offended her by being so glib.

"Oh, right. I'm sure it will all work out," I say.

She looks at me rather intently. "Do you understand what I mean?"

"About what?"

"About being in God's hands and in God's will."

I look into those soft, sober eyes and decide not to lie. "Not really. I don't think about God much."

"How do you live your life without considering God?"

Good question. "I don't know. I've done all right so far."

She smiles a little and shakes her head. "I don't understand. Who do you trust to watch over you, if not the Lord God?"

"I don't really trust anyone to watch over me."

"This is an idea I am not used to," she says quietly but with no judgment that I can discern.

"You probably grew up learning to trust God," I said.

"Yes. I never considered another way. Faith is part of my life, as much as breathing and walking."

"I guess that's the difference. My father never believed much of anything. My mother did when she was younger, but by the time I came along, she had given up a lot of her beliefs."

"So you were never taught. I'm so sorry." I can tell by her expression that she truly is sorry about my past.

"Maybe I'll learn to believe on my own someday."

Suddenly Mary takes in a sharp breath, giving a little cry that causes Joseph to stop the donkey.

"Mary?" He moves closer and holds her with such tenderness that I want to cry.

"Mother and the midwife told me about this. It starts slowly, and the pains are far apart at first. When they are close together, a few moments between, the baby will come."

"How many have come?" He places his hand on her belly.

"That was the first sharp one. I have ached for two days already. But that was the first sharp pain."

"Just a few more miles, just a few more, and we'll be

there." He strokes her pale face. For the moment I am invisible. They cling to each other and seem to gather more strength. Then Joseph steps out again, and the donkey moves slowly along the road. I stay beside Mary. I watch her face for sign of more pains, but she is still for quite a while. I get as close to her and the donkey as I can. As we make our way downhill on a winding curve, I hear Mary's voice. She is speaking softly again, not even look-ing at me.

"This isn't how I imagined it," she says. I see that there are tears in her eyes. "On the road like this. A baby should be born at home, with the grandmothers and aunts and neighbors all around. But this…" She gazes at the people in front of us. "I'll end up on the roadside, spread out on a blanket, surrounded by strangers. This just feels like a mis-take. This baby is…special. I hope we're doing everything the way we're supposed to."

I don't know what to say. I'm remembering the small room and the window and the angel I never saw. I'm remembering how Mary said yes to this huge thing promised to happen to her. I wonder if she even considered, months ago, that yes would mean this.

We get to Bethlehem, which is clearly not a big town, but it is teeming with people. They have come from around the country, carrying bags and children with them. The place is *full of noise and the smells of stirred-up walkways, of makeshift cooking fires in the olive and fig groves.*

Joseph leads us first to the home of his cousins. They greet him with great enthusiasm, but their happiness turns to anxiety when they see Mary. Mary and I stay on the path and watch Joseph talk with his relatives. He comes back to us, his face weary.

"They are already keeping four other families," he says. "They have them bedded down in every room, even in the garden. They gave me the name of the innkeeper just down this street. We'll look for a room there."

We go to the inn, which is already overflowing. Joseph leaves Mary and me in one of the stalls of the empty vegetable market and hurries away to seek any shelter he can find. We wait forever, while Mary passes through more sharp pains. She is off the donkey, resting as best she can on blankets on the ground, her legs and feet barely off the path that leads through the market stalls.

I see now, through the crowd, a familiar face—Grandpa! He's coming toward us. He recognizes me too.

Jana put down the journal abruptly. *I must be too tired to do this. There's no reason for Grandpa to show up in this story.* She wanted to put this away and just go for a walk, but that would mean walking downstairs, passing Mom in the family room, passing Aunt Cheryl. She looked at the journal. *So I'll just rewrite this and get rid of my grandparents.*

Then she remembered Sandra's mentioning that this exercise allowed the imagination to engage with the Bible story. Of course, this was her subconscious at work. She was in her grandparents' house, and she'd been listening to Mom talk about her grandparents. Maybe, deep down, she wanted to see them again, to get to know them now that she was grown. So they were appearing because...maybe she needed them to.

And why should she get rid of them? Wasn't this her story, something she was writing for her own reasons, in her own way? Wasn't that the point? In fact, there was no reason for *her* to be in the story either, yet here she was, a major character. She picked up the journal again.

Before I know what's happening, Grandpa is talking to Joseph, who has just arrived from another failed attempt to find lodging. Then Grandpa and Joseph help Mary onto the donkey, and Grandpa leads the beast with care through the crowded streets.

We come to a flat-roofed stone house that looks like all the other houses in the town. We go in the door and find the rooms full of people. Grandma comes to me and hugs me tightly. I'm so happy to see her that I find myself crying. Then she helps the men half carry, half lead Mary to some

cushions. Other people have to move in order for her to
sit down.

"We have a full house, as you can see," Grandpa says to
Joseph. "But there is room below, if you don't mind some of
the livestock for company."

Joseph looks anxiously at Mary, but Mary is beyond
anxious. She is in labor. She nods to Joseph.

"The heat from the animals keeps it warm, and there is
plenty of clean straw. Also, it is the only place here where the
young woman can have privacy when she births." Grandpa is
speaking, but Grandma stands at his elbow, nodding with
great emphasis.

"I'll help you, dear. And I've sent for the midwife. You'll
be just fine."

Down below? These houses have basements? Well, it
isn't exactly a basement, just a lower level where the livestock
is kept. It smells ripe and sweet, and the moment we're there I
sense the temperature rise. It's much warmer than the upper
level we just left. Standing in the shadows is a cow, also a
donkey. Two or three chickens scratch the straw-covered earth
floor.

I watch Grandma make a bed of blankets and fresh
straw. Mary lies down, her face damp and pale. After a few
moments, Grandma has chased everyone from the room but
the midwife and me. I hear Grandpa's and Joseph's voices

above us, muted by the noise of all the other visitors. There's the clank of utensils, the smell of bread and of onions and herbs cooking.

We've done all we can now. We can only wait for the pains to come and go, wait for this baby to arrive. Mary motions to me to lie beside her. I lower myself to the straw bed and cuddle up to her so she can lean back and rest against me. In front of us, her belly is a mound under the blanket.

"So often life doesn't go the way you think it will," she says between hard breaths. There's a tear in her voice. "You're given things to do that are too big for you. You're asked to believe things you don't even understand. You're forced to trust people you hardly know."

"Mary, are you scared?" I ask, because I realize that I am.

"Yes. Even though I trust God to bring this baby into the world, I'm scared. I have been afraid many times since all this began. I'm just a young woman, and so much is wrong in this world, and I fear that evil people and evil spirits will try to hurt my baby and me."

"You think God would let that happen?"

"No, not really. But feelings don't always go along with thoughts."

"You're right. Maybe we shouldn't listen to our feelings so much right now."

Another pain comes. And another. The night stretches out. Various women's faces appear at the entrance of the room as houseguests anxiously check to see if more help is needed. Joseph comes to Mary several times, but Grandma and now two other women gently turn him away.

The baby comes in the middle of the night. Mary and I both cry out, then sob with joy as the tiny human being makes his way to the rest of us. By then there is much blood, and I am drenched in sweat, mainly Mary's, because I have held on to her the whole time.

When Grandma cuts the cord and picks up the baby, she says, "Sweetheart, you have a healthy little boy," and we hear laughter in the room above us, along with hand clapping and relieved cries from women we don't even know. The entire household has gone through the night with us.

Joseph is beside Mary now, and he holds up his son, so tiny and contained in those large carpenter's hands.

"What will you call him?" Grandma's eyes are sparkling like stars.

Mary speaks. "Emmanuel—Jesus."

"Yes." Grandma is nodding wisely, happily. "God is with us."

The baby is washed and wrapped snugly in several strips of clean cloth. After he nurses for the first time, he falls asleep, and they place him in the manger, which is filled with *fresh straw. Grandma and her helpers declare that all is well, and they go upstairs to sleep at last. Grandma motions for me to follow, but Mary clasps my arm.*

"Thank you. I didn't expect to feel so scared—or to be so safe." She is so exhausted that her words slur. I hug her and leave as Joseph settles down beside her. Both of them will sleep until the baby wakes them, which won't be long from now, when he is hungry again.

Jana couldn't write anymore. She was exhausted too. She'd become so involved in this story that the room around her smelled like hay. She expected to see that other Mary here in the bed, with a baby resting against her.

She went downstairs, where Mom slept while Fred Astaire danced energetically in complete silence. Mom must have pushed the Mute button during a commercial. Jana took the remote gently from her mother's hand and surfed channels for a while. She found soap operas, game shows, famous judges sniping at real-life plaintiffs and defendants. A faded Western offered cowboys in amazingly clean clothes and hats, their horses pounding through wilderness. In some Christmas movie, a nerdy looking boy dreamed of a Red Ryder BB gun. A goofy family show from the seventies presented some dilemma related to sisters liking the same boy at school.

She watched all of this but in her mind watched Mary and the baby sleep. She wandered upstairs to study her grandparents' faces on the wall of the hallway.

Then she went to the bathroom and studied her own face in the mirror while she washed her hands.

So often life doesn't go the way you think it will. You're given things to do that are too big for you. You're asked to believe things you don't even understand. You're forced to trust people you hardly know.

She stared harder at the face in the mirror and realized that the girl in there was crying.

*E*vening came early, invading the already quiet house. Tomorrow would be Christmas Eve, and Aunt Cheryl appeared to be conserving her energy for what would be a busy day. Mom rested, rousing after dark to eat a bit of soup and then visit with them in the sitting room. She was looking better now, more lively, a person with emotions living inside her. Jana remained with her mother and aunt, content to talk about nothing in particular. Tonight she felt lonely. At first she thought it was just a residual longing for Gary, but it went much deeper than that. She dreaded going up to her room and being faced with nothing but worry over Mom and anxiety about how the holiday would go.

Finally, she was the only one who hadn't gone to bed. She watched television until eleven, then trudged up to her room. She plopped into bed and opened the journal automatically.

In the middle of the night, I hear a thudding sound and some voices. They are male voices, just outside. I come wide awake then, because I remember what Mary said about people coming to harm her and the baby. I slip down to the lower level and see that Mary is sitting up straight, the baby clutched to her, and Joseph is at the door that leads directly outside from the stable.

"My wife has just given birth. What could you want at this time of night?" Joseph sounds irritated, but I imagine a note of fear as well.

"The baby—yes, that's why we've come. We've heard about this baby, and we want to see him."

Mary holds little Jesus tighter. I sit down beside her. I look toward the upstairs entrance, hoping that someone else is awake, that Grandpa and some of the men are up and ready to get rid of these strangers.

"What do you want with a baby?" Joseph's voice is sharp now and threatening.

"We were told he would be born tonight."

"Who told you?"

There is an awkward silence. I can hear the rustle of the

cow in the stall nearby and the breathing of the infant making tiny sleep sounds against his mother.

Now I can see four or five men in the entrance. I see two or three boys as well. From the smell of them, I guess they deal with goats and sheep.

"The angels told us." It is a boy's voice. The men's eyes dart to Joseph and then to the youngster who has blurted out the answer. Then one of them clears his throat.

"It's true, what the boy said. We were just over those hills," he says, motioning behind him, "with our flocks. That's all we were doing. And out of nowhere came lights and singing." His voice is trembling. "We're telling the truth, sir. There were angels—many of them. They filled the sky. I'm surprised you didn't hear them yourself. We thought the whole town would be up and about. They told us we would find the child swaddled and in a manger. Otherwise we would never have found the little one with all the crowds who are in Bethlehem tonight."

"What did the angels tell you about my son?" Mary's eyes are wide open, and she strokes the fine hair on her baby's head. The baby is awake, trying to focus his eyes. He makes infant murmurs but doesn't cry.

Another man steps forward. I can tell by his manner that he is embarrassed to be in this strange home, in town. He knows he has stepped far outside his place. But the look on his face is bright, even happy. He takes another step, trying to see Mary's son.

"The angel said, 'I bring you good news of great joy for everyone! The Savior—yes, the Messiah, the Lord—has been born tonight in Bethlehem, the city of David! And this is how you will recognize him: You will find a baby lying in a manger, wrapped snugly in strips of cloth!' "

"Then there were many, many other angels," another shepherd breaks in, "singing, 'Glory to God in the highest heaven, and peace on earth to all whom God favors.' "

As they speak, the small group edges closer to us. They remind me of children trying to take in the sight of gifts. When they see the child, one by one they kneel down. The boys are grinning; the men are crying. They don't take their eyes off Mary and the baby.

I notice that Mary and Joseph are looking at each other, a mixture of emotions in their gazes. I'm waiting to hear Joseph's response to this story of angels in the sky. Joseph seems to be the pragmatic type, a man who will always do the right thing but who has little patience for foolishness. I expect him to grab one of the men by the coat and toss all of them out. But after gazing into Mary's face for several moments, Joseph moves toward one of the boys. He kneels down with the child and places an arm across the small shoulders.

"We were told that others would know about him too,"
he says quietly.

Mary scoots forward and loosens the clutch she's had on
her son. She lays him across the blankets that are over her
lap, turns him to face the motley group in front of us.

"May I touch him?" the smallest boy asks. He is thin
and smudged with grime, but his eyes are large and fairly
glowing.

"Of course." Mary takes the boy's hand in hers and with
it traces lightly across the baby's cheek. "He's brand-new and
very soft." She is smiling, and the smile looks so old and wise
that I can't take my eyes off of her.

The other boys touch the baby timidly, but the men
merely smile and remain on their knees.

We stay like that for maybe a few moments, or maybe it's
an hour. I have no sense of time now. I watch Mary, still torn
open from birth, exhausted and full of questions, offering her
presence to these strangers. I watch Joseph sit to the side, his
mouth slightly open as if he's in a trance. He watches Mary;
he watches the newborn make faces and gurgle, still too new
to see the present world as it is.

"So gracious you are, good people," one of the shepherds
says as he stands finally and pulls the youngsters to their feet.
"We will remember this night for the rest of our lives. We'll
remember the babe, and we'll thank God for your kindness."

They are gone. Joseph shuts the door and comes back to Mary and the baby. He kneels close, touches the infant's cheek with a finger, and leans toward the small dark eyes.

"Little child, sweet baby," Joseph croons, his eyes shining. "Do you know how special you are? You're too young to understand how dangerous it is to leave sheep unguarded in the hills. The wolves come. They come to kill and destroy the flock."

"Maybe God protected the sheep while he led their shepherds here," Mary says just as softly.

Joseph rises then and pulls his coat around him. "I need to walk, Mary. You're all right, aren't you?"

"We're fine. Go take your walk."

I start to return upstairs, but Mary reaches for me. "Don't. I'm not afraid, but I want company." Her expression holds much that I can't describe. "My mother isn't here; no one I know is with me. Can I talk to you, Mary?"

"Yes." I sit down, and both of us watch the baby, who has returned to sleep, unaware that anything strange has occurred here tonight.

"You believe those shepherds, don't you?" I ask.

She doesn't look at me but nods. "I have the feeling that angels are going to keep appearing in this child's life. One came to Joseph in a dream; otherwise he wouldn't have married me or believed what I told him about the pregnancy."

I'd forgotten about that. So far I've not paid much attention to Joseph. But I realize now that just as much faith is required from him as from Mary. He said yes too. He trusted too. What a way to begin a marriage, caught up in some mysterious connection between God and his own young wife.

"This is a special child, set apart by God to do wonderful things." She glances at me then. "Do <u>you</u> believe the shepherds?"

"I suppose. How else could that bunch have found you and the baby?"

She is looking at me, questions in her eyes. It occurs to me that she is hoping my faith can help hers as much as I'm depending on hers to help mine. I'm aware then that even I have a faith to call my own.

"And they didn't ask for anything," I said. "They just wanted to see the baby. And once they had, they were satisfied and went back to the hills."

I see now that Mary's eyes are glistening. "What has God done to me, Mary? What is in store? How do I live from one day to the next when I know that all of this is outside my own power, that I'm a very small part of a very large plan?"

"I don't know."

"We have to remember what happened tonight—every detail." *Her gaze is intense.* "Promise me that someday—

when you doubt everything about God—you will remember
me and the baby and Joseph and the shepherds. Promise me
that you'll remember the angels."

"I will."

"And that you'll believe in the One who is somehow
watching over all of this."

I pause. Mary is asking me to believe in her God.

"Someone who brought all of us together, Someone who
created this beautiful child."

Can I believe in Someone? It's not as if such a belief
would take the place of another belief. For me, there has never
been Someone, or anyone.

"Yes, I will. I don't understand though."

She laughs at me now. It's not a hushed, middle-of-the-
night laugh of a young girl trying to remain inconspicuous.
Mary's face breaks open, and she throws her head back and
laughs loudly. She looks at my bewilderment and laughs until
tears run down her face. I hear people above us shifting,
roused by the sound.

"Oh, it hurts!" she says, holding her abdomen because
the laughing is jostling her too much. But she keeps laughing
and looks at me. "What's to understand? I haven't understood
anything since the day this began. That's why you believe in
One who is wiser than you! You do the believing, and God
takes care of the understanding."

*Neither do I understand why all this is so funny to
Mary. But she is making some sense. Maybe I do put too
much importance on understanding.*

Jana read what she'd just written. "My own characters are
preaching at me." She snapped the journal shut but noticed the
used tissues decorating the lamp table. The scene with the
shepherds got to her. She hadn't expected that. What really
jarred her was Joseph talking about wolves. She was familiar
enough with the life of Jesus to know that the wolves got him
eventually.

THE GIFT

*T*he next day was Christmas Eve. Jana lay in bed at seven in the morning and listened to the sounds of Mom and Aunt Cheryl downstairs. They were having coffeecake and tea in the kitchen, their voices floating up through the floor register near Jana's bed. The women were planning the day's events, which consisted mainly of cooking and decorating. Their conversation was calm, but its energy brought to mind memories of past Christmases when Jana was small and would awaken to the smell of breakfast and the astounding realization that relatives would come that day, their arms full of presents. Back then she was always listening for clues in the grownups' voices. She could tell from the inflections alone what time of day it was and whether or not life in the house was going well. She could hear the stress or the excitement before her ears could pick out words. She woke up to those voices and fell asleep to them. They were always humming in the background of her life, forming sense and safety.

In the quiet of the bedroom she felt, just for a moment, that old safety as Mom and Aunt Cheryl talked in the room below about the day's logistics. She decided to hold on to that feeling as much as she could all day long.

Later the two women wandered in and out of the kitchen, dealing with last batches of cookies and quick breads. When they weren't dealing with food, they were arranging wreaths and baskets of fruit, elaborate table settings, and strings of lights.

"Why don't you take charge of the big buffet in the dining room?" Mom motioned toward the solid cabinet of dark walnut. "Set all the sweets over there. In the top drawer are crystal candleholders and some burgundy tapers."

"Okay." Jana put all the trays and tins on the dining room table and studied the space on the buffet. This gave her the opportunity to notice in more detail the collection of family pictures that sat along the back of the buffet. These photos were more recent than those in the upstairs hallway. Grandma and Grandpa appeared in their later years, grandchildren around them. Jana's high school graduation picture stood there, along with school pictures of other kids in the extended family. Mom and Aunt Cheryl were depicted as the older women they were, in casual shots taken on the patio some recent summer. Their brother, Uncle Jason, posed with his wife and daughters in a formal portrait. Dad was in a couple of the group pictures. The wedding picture of Dad and Mom had been removed and a portrait of cousin Susan's new baby added. Susan was only three years older than Jana.

Jana was lost in the faces when Mom walked up beside her and said close to Jana's ear, "Your college graduation picture will make it there as soon as we remember to buy a frame."

"No big deal."

"I thought by now I'd have a picture of you and Gary. How is he?"

Jana's mouth went dry. She and Gary had broken up after Mom moved south. With so much else going on, Jana had decided that Mom didn't need to know about one more of life's upheavals.

"He's okay," she said but could feel Mom's stare, a strong beam on the side of her face.

"You've not mentioned him. I haven't noticed you calling him either."

So. Mom had figured this out already.

"We broke up."

"Oh, honey." A hand rested on Jana's shoulder. "I'm so sorry. When?"

"A few weeks ago." She stared at the floral sconce on the wall above the buffet, not wanting to see the hurt in Mom's eyes. There'd been a time when she told Mom just about everything. Jana couldn't pinpoint a reason, but talk between them hadn't come easily for a while. "It wasn't a big surprise, just took me forever to make up my mind."

"He didn't hurt you, did he?"

"No, but I don't think he really loved me either."

Mom was quiet for a moment. "Well, it's better to figure that out now. No wonder you're depressed." She left the room, and Jana realized they'd had this entire conversation without looking at each other. When did it get so difficult, being related to another person?

*S*everal times people dropped in to bring gifts and greetings. At two in the afternoon, Uncle Jason and the cousins stopped by, including Susan and her eighteen-month-old, Travis. Jana (who remained Mary Georgianna throughout this visit) held Travis for as long as he'd allow it, then visited with Susan, noticing more about her than on previous visits. She observed her cousin's motherhood—the hands that were always close enough to grab Travis away from a sharp coffee-table corner, the eyes that monitored him constantly while Susan carried on a conversation. Jana wished they could stay all evening, but this year they would spend Christmas Eve with the other side of the family, Uncle Jason's in-laws in Athens, where Aunt Rena was now.

"Bye, Mary Georgianna!" That was Bridget, Susan's fourteen-year-old sister, who was old enough to admire people like Jana who had been to college and lived in places like Chicago. Jana watched Bridget, Susan, Travis, and Uncle Jason get into the car and wave as they left. Susan's husband, Pete, was a medical resident and on call throughout the holiday. Yet the family was all together, in its own way. They were healthy;

they seemed happy. Jana wondered if they thought about this, if they stopped to recognize how good life was for them.

After supper, Jana, Mom, and Aunt Cheryl put on warm slacks and bright sweaters and went to church for the late-night Christmas Eve service. Whether due to fatigue or resignation, Jana settled into the pew and decided that she might enjoy herself. Maybe a part of her, some part left over from long ago, really did want decorations and music and other Christmasy things. The large sanctuary felt cozy, its ceiling lights dimmed and a taper flickering in each window. The air smelled of evergreen and candle wax.

Aunt Cheryl leaned toward Jana and said, "Usually we just have Scripture readings and sing carols. But the Sunday school children are acting out the nativity. They were supposed to do it last Sunday morning, but Joseph and two of the shepherds came down with the twenty-four-hour flu."

"Oh, I love to watch the kids." Mom's face glowed with the light from nearby candles, which made her appear almost healthy.

As a girl read the Christmas story from the book of Luke, a little pageant unfolded involving children and someone's baby doll. Laughter rippled through the pews when Mary picked up the doll from the manger and put it on her shoulder, and there was a mechanical cry, "Mama!" Apparently the baby Jesus was one of those talking dolls. In her surprise, Mary almost dropped Jesus. The shepherds, their bathrobes dragging the floor, started shaking with laughter. The angel, glitter halo tilting toward one ear, looked distressed and motioned to Mary to put the baby back in the manger. The narrator, about twelve and nervous to be reading in public, didn't even notice the commotion.

After the wise men had presented their gifts, the angel invited people in the congregation to sing the hymns listed in their programs. So they sang seven or eight carols in a row. As her eyes scanned verses about Bethlehem, angels, and a holy night, Jana's memory flashed the scenes inside her mind. For the first time, the familiar phrases seemed personal. The words tugged at her, and she felt lightheaded several times. She was relieved when the singing was over and they headed to the adjoining hall for refreshments.

Jana stood near Mom, hoping to exist easily in that circle without having to say much. She noticed Sandra talking to a couple of teenagers a few yards away. Sandra looked up and saw her and smiled.

"Hey! Merry Christmas."

"Merry Christmas."

"How is your visit going?" Of course she would never say something like, "How is your depression going?"

"Fine."

Sandra had moved away from the others and stood next to

Jana. She lowered her voice. "How were the test results from the doctor?"

"Everything's okay." Jana took a drink of cider. "I'm having some fun with the writing."

"Good!" Sandra's smile was so easy, so not pushy. "Come over sometime after the holiday if you like, and tell me about it."

"I will. Thanks." She wanted to say more but wasn't sure what. Maybe she just liked standing near Sandra in that small realm of ease that surrounded the woman.

*O*nce home and in bed, Jana decided to read past the Christmas story. She read Luke 2:21-40. Then she held the pen above the journal page, waiting for something to happen.

A few weeks later Mary and Joseph take the baby to the temple in Jerusalem. It is time for them to offer the sacrifice for purification. I want to ask Mary about this, because it is such a strange custom, but she is preoccupied with bathing the baby and getting ready for this appointment.

"I wish I understood this sacrifice business. It seems so primitive," I comment. Joseph is with Grandpa and some other men. They talk in the mornings about human affairs,

politics, whatever. Some things are the same everywhere. On the way to the temple, Joseph and Mary will purchase doves for the sacrifice.

"Primitive?" Mary's right eyebrow arches a little.

"I'm not used to thinking about God that way—someone who requires sacrifice."

"Everything requires a sacrifice. In order to do one thing, you must give up something else. Isn't that right?"

I can't think of a good answer to that.

"A child is a gift, a blessing. When we offer a sacrifice, we are saying in a way people can see that we acknowledge God's goodness."

"And if you don't make a sacrifice? What will God do to you?"

She looks startled. The baby is squirming as she swaddles him. He doesn't look too happy to be wrapped up like that. "If I don't make the sacrifice, I have offended myself, not God. I have not expressed what is truly inside me." She frowns a little. "How do you demonstrate that you are grateful?"

"I say thank you."

"A few words."

"Yes, but I mean them."

She laughs then, a habit I've noticed. She has learned

already that she can't be serious about everything all the time. "I know you do. Let's not worry about customs, all right? You'll come, won't you?"

I have never understood why Mary wants me around. She appears to know what she needs to do and when. I can't imagine this girl ever needing advice. But at times she walks up to me, her eyes prying into my soul, and says something, for the purpose of seeing my reaction and thus judging whether or not she's all right. Just yesterday we were sitting in the courtyard, enjoying a letup in the rain, cuddling the baby in the fresh air. She leaned toward me, and I could see the wheels turning in her head.

"I wonder what he knows already."

She was talking about Jesus. I looked at the baby, still tiny and for the most part sleepy.

"What I mean is, will he be different from other babies? Will he understand things sooner?"

I kept looking at the baby. He appeared to be just a normal infant. "I don't know."

"And if he is very wise, will he need me?"

So this was the real question, the one causing disturbance in an otherwise calm girl. Would Jesus need her? I took the baby from her arms and looked at him carefully.

"Of course he'll need you. Babies and children need their

mothers. If he weren't going to need you, then he wouldn't have been born. He would have just appeared, full grown or something."

Her eyes got wide at this idea. "Oh, I see what you mean. It's important for him to be little and to grow. And—" She stopped, and that worried look filled her face, the one that appears when she has just realized a new wrinkle in her life. "And not only will he need a mother and a father, he will need the very best mother and father." She shook her head. "What was that angel thinking?"

"From what you said, it wasn't the angel's idea; he was just the messenger. What you mean is, what was God thinking?"

"Shh!" Her worry turned into alarm. "Don't question God! Don't ever do that!"

"Why not? How can God give answers if there are no questions?"

She took back little Jesus. "I was not taught to question almighty God."

"You weren't taught that almighty God would make you pregnant either." Maybe I shouldn't have been so direct, but my friend Mary has a lot to learn. She'd better get used to asking _lots_ of questions. In fact, it wouldn't hurt if she learned to argue really well, because her life will never be normal, and people will never understand her. This was my impression anyway. I didn't mention any of this; it seemed that I'd said enough already.

So I am surprised that she still wants me to come along today to this holy event. I can't go into the temple proper, not being a Jew. But I will accompany them to the outer courtyard.

Joseph comes in, and the three of us, with the baby, go on our way, borrowing a donkey cart from the relatives to take us the few miles into Jerusalem. Just outside the temple are stalls where sacrificial animals are sold. Joseph buys two turtle-doves. They're in a cage, and the man takes them somewhere out of sight and kills them and then hands them limp to Joseph, streaks of blood on the soft feathers. I try not to look at them or think about any of this.

We are walking toward the outer courtyard when a man approaches us. He looks really old, but his face is full of energy.

"Dear lady," he says, coming directly to Mary. He peers at the baby in her arms. "May I see the child?"

Mary is startled, but after staring at the man for a second or two, she holds the baby toward him. He reaches out and takes Jesus. Out of the corner of my eye I can see Joseph twitch, wanting to do something but unsure what that should be.

"I am Simeon," the man says. He is holding the baby as

if he does this all the time. His thin, white hands gently grasp the bundle. He brings his face so close to the baby that his white beard rests on the swaddling. The baby looks right up into the ancient face. I follow the gaze and see that tears are sliding down Simeon's cheeks.

> "Lord, now I can die in peace!
>> As you promised me,
> I have seen the Savior
>> you have given to all people.
> He is a light to reveal God to the nations,
>> and he is the glory of your people Israel!"

He raises Jesus into the air as he makes these pronouncements. Mary and Joseph stare at him, then at each other. After a majestic pause, Simeon hands Jesus back to Mary. She takes the baby, and the old gentleman pats her arm.

"The Holy Spirit led me here today. The Spirit said some time ago that I would not die until I saw the Messiah. As you can see"—he stops to smile, his eyes glittering—"I'm an old man who should have been dead by now. I have been ready to meet my God, but I wanted only to see his promise. Today I have." He reaches to pull Joseph in, and they make a small circle, the three of them, the baby in their center.

"The Lord bless you," Simeon says, his voice deep and

surprisingly strong for his age. He continues to grasp Mary's arm. He looks into her face until she returns his gaze.

"This child will be rejected by many in Israel, and it will be their undoing. But he will be the greatest joy to many others. Thus, the deepest thoughts of many hearts will be revealed."

Mary does not take her gaze from Simeon. Joseph, too, is staring, motionless.

Simeon's voice becomes hoarse as he looks more intently into Mary's eyes. "And a sword will pierce your very soul." They stay there, still as ever, until finally Mary nods to Simeon as if to say she understands.

Another voice causes us to look up. "Praise God! O, praise the Lord of heaven and earth!"

We look toward the sound and see an elderly woman hurrying toward us, her arms in the air, triumphant. (Does she look a lot like Myrtle?) She comes right up to us.

"He's the Messiah, is he not?" She looks at Mary and Joseph and then at Simeon, who smiles broadly.

"Yes, Anna, it is he."

"Ah, the Lord has revealed it to this old woman. I've been a widow for so long, devoted to God alone. And he has rewarded my many years with this one moment."

Simeon is laughing, a shaky old man's laugh, as he watches her. He turns to Joseph and says, "We have witnessed Anna's prayer and fasting in this temple for a generation or more. I'm not at all surprised that the Holy Spirit would reveal this child to her."

He pats the baby's face once more and then walks away.

Anna strokes Jesus' cheek, then leans forward to kiss Mary's. She says nothing but turns to leave. She sees me then and stops. She doesn't say anything, just smiles. I smile back, but the muscles in my face are trembling because suddenly I am on the spot. Am I supposed to say something? Then Anna takes a step toward me and speaks.

"You have seen what very few people will ever see."

"I know."

"God bless you, child." She quickly leaves then, as if she must do many things today, as if she's not an old woman at all but just born into the world herself.

Mary and Joseph silently walk forward, leaving me in the courtyard.

While I wait, I watch people. There are so many, and most of them look worried or angry or tired. I realize that crowds are like that—not many smiles or much laughter. I think about the happiness that radiated from Simeon and Anna. It's strange that they recognized Jesus while all these other people didn't. What does that mean? Are the two who see the truth really crazy in some way? Or is everyone else simply in the dark?

I wonder, then, what I look like in a crowd. Would I ever recognize the Jesus child? Would I know what to look for? Would I care enough to notice?

When Mary and Joseph return, Jesus is sleeping peacefully once more. I can see that Mary has been crying. I don't know if she's upset by the encounters with Simeon and Anna or if something about the sacrifice has caused this. Maybe she's just tired from trying to figure it all out. I walk close to her.

"Are you all right?" I ask.

"You ask me that a lot. Do I always seem to be ill or in trouble?"

"No, but you're always going through events that would traumatize anyone else."

She laughs lightly but doesn't answer.

"Pretty strange," I begin. "Simeon and Anna."

"Yes, but now I expect strange things to happen." There's sadness in her eyes.

"What do you think he meant—about the sword in your heart?"

"The sword piercing my soul? I don't know. I don't want to know. I don't have to know that now."

"I suppose it's good to be warned."

"It's not good or bad. It just is." There's a sharpness to her voice. I've hit a nerve.

"Do you…know what Simeon was talking about?"

Joseph glances at us. I suspect that he eavesdrops on us most of the time.

"There are prophecies," Mary says. "It's difficult to know which ones are meant for Jesus. But there are prophecies about suffering."

"But for now we think about living," Joseph breaks in. He's looking meaningfully at me. "We are given a child to bring up in the fear of the Lord. We will do what is best to do."

"Yes." Mary's voice is a whisper.

We get into the cart for our return to Bethlehem.

"Everyone suffers," Joseph says. He is looking down the street we are traveling. Jerusalem is a busy place, and people pass us, busy with their own affairs. "Everyone. We will all suffer. The question is, how will we suffer? Will it make us angry, fearful, hateful? Or will we respond with wisdom and patience?"

I realize that Joseph is looking at me again.

"What do we do when we are suffering? What kind of people do we become? That is our main concern. God must deal with the rest."

This is the longest speech I have heard this man make. But when he finally talks, he definitely has something to say.

"You're right," I say. "I shouldn't have ruined this day with my worrying."

"You didn't ruin anything," says Mary. "We're all figuring out how to think, what to say, how to act. We'll be fine." She looks at me. "You'll be fine too."

The bedside clock said two in the morning. Jana put the journal aside. She wasn't sleepy, just weary. She went quietly to the kitchen and heated water in the microwave for a cup of tea. She opened one of the cookie tins and took her snack to the living room. Moonlight flowed through the sheer curtains of the picture window, streaming across the sofa like a scarf. Jana sat there in the light, allowing the teacup to warm her hands.

"Well, Mary," she whispered to the still room, "I can enter your story and walk with you. But I wish someone could walk with me."

I'm right here.

She knew it was her imagination talking, but she knew it was also Mary, fresh from history, stepping off some timeless path.

She thought that maybe if she kept whispering into the moonlight, the conversation would feel more real. "Joseph said that everybody suffers."

Yes.

"And you said that I'll be fine."

The Lord cares for each of us.

"How did you know things would work out?"

I didn't know anything. I could only trust.

"I have trouble with that."

Don't we all.

They sat on the sofa and watched the shadows flicker as wind moved through tree branches outside.

Mary. The voice paused in the way a speaker waits for the audience to look up and listen. *Suffering does not mean that you aren't loved.*

The air around her seemed to come alive, and Jana's heart made a funny lurch.

We went through all that for a reason, you know. He came to us for a reason.

"Was he wonderful, the way they say he was?" Blood pulsed in Jana's head, and she listened hard for Mary's reply.

Yes, but he was never what any of us expected.

"I wish I'd lived back then. Maybe trust would have been easier if I'd actually met him."

It wouldn't have been easier. And you can meet him anytime you want.

Then the house fell so completely still that Jana imagined an invisible audience waited for her to speak. She finally got the words out. "Every step we take is some kind of lesson, isn't it?"

Mary, your whole life is a revelation.

She cuddled up in the pillows on the sofa and put her face deep into them so no one could hear her cry. A great kindness overwhelmed the room. And Jana recognized the young woman in her mind to be a separate entity, something beyond what she had created. Through some inexplicable process, imagination had opened a door to something else. She couldn't undo it or rewrite it. But she had stepped through the opening and was standing in a different place now. What was it Mary had said? *There was so much joy. I think that is how a person feels when she is in the presence of God. I was so happy, so unafraid, so eager for my life to happen, so sure that everything would be fine.*

In a little while, her tears stopped. She looked at the clock and realized it was Christmas morning. She returned to bed and fell asleep quickly, feeling more peaceful than she had in a very long time.

*M*om woke up before dawn, so sick that they took her to the emergency room. She couldn't stop vomiting. The doctor on call gave her a shot for the nausea. Mom settled down, but her color was awful—or, rather, nonexistent. Her eyes were dull. Within the hour she was in a semiprivate room on the third floor. An IV had been put in her thin arm, which already carried the marks of many needles and small bruises of various colors.

Jana sat at the bedside and watched her mother's features.

Your whole life is a revelation. What about Mom's life? What revelation was coming now, what new thing to deal with? As much as Jana tried to argue with God, or Mary, or whoever, her heart wasn't in it. Her impulse was to ask why, but that didn't seem to be the right question anymore. *What kind of people will we become?* She remembered Joseph's clear eyes. How could he have known how much—and how soon—she would need *that* question?

Aunt Cheryl sat with her as the sun came up and shone on the sterile surfaces of the room. She got up and pulled the curtains to block the light from Mom's face.

"You two go on home," Mom said. Her eyes were closed; Jana had assumed she was sleeping.

"Oh no, we're fine right here," said Aunt Cheryl.

"We have company coming in a few hours for dinner. You can't just cancel."

Jana had forgotten about this. Another family from church was joining them, along with Myrtle.

"It's not like they're traveling miles to be here," Jana said, moving closer to Mom. "They're right in the neighborhood, and they'll understand."

"What can you do here? I need to sleep, that's all. It was just a vomiting spell—that happens sometimes. After I rest, I'll be fine. They may even let me go home later this afternoon."

Aunt Cheryl sat on the hospital bed. "Are you sure? Mary

Georgianna's right—we don't have to do dinner today. The food will keep, and everyone will come another day."

"I *really* want you to go home and have dinner." Mom patted Aunt Cheryl's hand. Aunt Cheryl put her other hand on top of Mom's.

"All right. That's what we'll do. You rest. I'll call later, and if you feel like eating, we'll bring the feast to you."

Mom smiled, quite satisfied. Jana left the room with Aunt Cheryl, but her whole body filled with fear. "Should we be doing this?"

Aunt Cheryl took Jana's arm. "Yes. Will you help me cook?"

"If you give me really good instructions."

Jana got lost in chopping and stirring for the next three hours. They set the table. The guests arrived—Mark and Carolyn from church, with their four-year-old, Daniel. The parents put the boy between them to contain his energy somewhat. Myrtle sat on the other side of the table, next to Jana. Aunt Cheryl was at one end of the table, Mom's empty chair at the opposite end.

Jana was too unsettled to make much adult conversation, so she engaged Daniel from time to time. He was a friendly little boy, a bit shy at first but more talkative as dinner went on. Aunt Cheryl and Mark and Carolyn maintained most of the conversation. Myrtle, who had been so animated a few days ago, was quiet but peaceful. Jana felt some comfort in

Myrtle's sitting beside her. She watched the old hands pass dishes and butter bread. These hands had been through a lot. They reminded Jana of the hands of the elderly prophetess outside the temple.

Then, while Mark took Daniel to the living room to look at the Christmas tree and Carolyn and Aunt Cheryl cleared the table, Myrtle turned to Jana.

"I'm sorry your mother's not here. I know she looked forward to having her Christmas dinner with you this year."

"I should probably be at the hospital with her now, instead of celebrating."

Myrtle dismissed the idea with a shake of her head. "If we put off celebrations until everything was fine, we'd all starve and never eat another piece of pecan pie."

"If your mother were in the hospital, where would *you* be?" Jana wasn't trying to be difficult; she really wanted to know.

"I've buried both my mother and my father, a sister and two brothers." Myrtle's voice quivered slightly. "And I have celebrated the Christmas feast every year of my life, sometimes with my tears adding extra salt to the turkey and dressing." She looked at Jana, her eyes dry. "This is what faith gives us, celebrations of what has already come true and celebrations of what will someday be true. We're between the promises and the coming true. And to keep us going, the Good Lord gives us celebrations. We celebrate because we believe, not because we're particularly happy, because often we're not." She smiled then, and Jana recognized the face of Anna. One wrinkled hand, cool and soft, rested on Jana's for a moment. "You are exactly where you should be, my dear. If your mother were dying, your place would be at her bedside. But she is not dying—she's just sick. And if she needed your help, she would ask for it."

Jana took a deep breath, hoping to absorb some of Anna's steadiness.

"So let's get ourselves ready to eat pie." Myrtle was up and standing in the kitchen doorway. She called out to Aunt Cheryl, asking where the dessert plates were located.

They were still hovering over pie when the phone rang. Jana was nearest the kitchen doorway, so she picked up the call in there.

"Is this my Jana? It's Dad."

"Hi, Dad," she said, moving farther into the kitchen for privacy. "Merry Christmas."

"Merry Christmas. Your visit going all right?"

"Fine." No point in bringing up Mom's stay in the hospital. Dad had no room left for Mom's burdens. "We just had dinner."

"The car's ready for you. We brought it here to the house. You're flying in Sunday, right?"

"Yeah."

An awkward silence followed. She sensed Dad struggling at the other end. Finally he spoke. "We're really glad you spent Thanksgiving with us, honey."

His voice sounded so mournful, lonely even. A sudden sadness welled up in Jana. Dad was trying so hard. Right then, she missed him.

"Thanks for having me," she said. "And for helping with the car and everything."

"Anytime you want to come out here, you just say the word, and we'll get your tickets, okay?"

"Maybe this summer. I'd like to go hiking." She'd not thought about hiking until this moment, but she wanted to say something that would ease the pain she heard in his voice.

"Oh, the hiking's great here. That'd be great, honey. Tell your mom and everybody else Merry Christmas, okay?"

After their company had left, she and Aunt Cheryl visited Mom. She was doing better but wasn't interested in food. The doctor planned to release her in the morning. Her color was better, and she had rested well during the afternoon. Jana could feel her own panic begin to subside.

For the first time since Jana had arrived, Aunt Cheryl seemed truly tired, so Jana drove them home and insisted on finishing the kitchen cleanup on her own. Aunt Cheryl thanked her with a hug and then disappeared. Jana looked out the window above the sink while her hands sloshed through the warm water. It was too dark to see much, but several trees in the backyard stood out in silhouette against the glow of the neighbors' Christmas lights. She thought of the trees on Dad's place, remembered the house and the little valley it sat in. It wouldn't be so bad to go back. She really should make a point of visiting. The divorce was an ugly reality, but at least Dad still wanted her in his life. She'd had friends in high school and college who weren't so lucky, who'd been left behind like so much outdated furniture.

*S*he had now searched all four gospels for any other glimpses of this Christ story. Tonight she found an event in Matthew that was not recorded anywhere else.

I'm no longer in my grandparents' house, but I am still in Bethlehem, in another house, another room. Mary again is near a window, at a table, cutting vegetables. She looks different, older maybe. Then I see why, because a small child, about two years old, runs into Mary's legs, grabbing her long skirt and shrieking.

"Oh!" Mary's face opens up happily as she looks down at her son. At her expression and exclamation, Jesus laughs, that totally delighted laugh only children can deliver.

"Oh!" Mary says again, eliciting another round of

laughter. Mary cuts off a small piece of cucumber and offers it to the toddler. Jesus takes it and runs over to a pallet on the floor and studies his food as he eats.

Mary sees me then. She drops the knife on the table and comes to give me a hug.

"You've come! I've been waiting for you."

"You have?"

"Isn't he growing?"

I look at the child on the mat. "He sure is. Such a happy boy."

"He laughs so much, and then he'll be quiet for a long time, as though he's studying something inside himself."

I make a point of looking at her eyes, and I find the same calm but more brightness than before. Motherhood agrees with her.

"Everything has gone all right?" I ask.

"Yes." She goes back to the vegetables. "We decided to stay in Bethlehem. Joseph's cousins helped us find this place."

"Why didn't you go back to Nazareth?"

She doesn't answer right away. "It's too difficult to go back to where people have always known us. We heard that stories had already gone ahead of us."

"What stories?"

"Well, the shepherds who came that night told everybody they saw what the angels had said. And the prophecies of

Simeon and Anna circulated quickly. I would expect people to discount what shepherds said, but they have been hesitant to speak against their own elders. Simeon died, you know, just a month after we met him at the temple."

"And people back home—do they believe any of this?"

"They don't know what to think. And we don't know what to expect, what may happen next. Joseph worries that people will call us crazy if we speak honestly about our son. Worse, some may try to harm us if they think we are speaking blasphemy."

"Maybe you shouldn't tell anyone about Jesus or the prophecies."

"For the most part we don't. Here and there a person appears who will recognize Jesus. Just when life begins to feel normal, someone stops me in the market or knocks at the door, and I never know whether to bring the child out or to run and hide him."

"But everything else is all right?"

"Yes! I love being a mother! Every day is a present to open. What will he say or do? What will we discover together?"

"How is Joseph?"

"I never imagined that fatherhood could make a good man an even better man, but it has. Our life here is good, and my family has come to see us several times."

We hear men's voices; I recognize one as Joseph's. There is a shuffle, and I see him at the door. I greet him, and his face lights up, but I can see that something has happened.

"Mary," he says. "Someone is here to see the child."

Then I hear more commotion outside. Many voices, many steps, the snorting of animals.

"Who?" A shadow crosses Mary's face.

"Come see."

Mary turns to me. "Watch the baby. I want to see first before I take him outside."

I go to the pallet, where Jesus is rubbing two little twigs together, studying them with wonder.

Several moments pass, and then Mary and Joseph return. Joseph picks up the baby, and he and Mary stand before the open door, waiting. I can't take the suspense and go to the door and look outside.

I see then what all the noise is about. At the edge of the yard, and spilling into the street, is a caravan like nothing I've ever seen. There must be twenty camels and half that many men. They aren't dressed like anyone around here. In fact, several of them appear to be important, because their clothing is lavish and full of colors—the kind of clothing worn by royalty. They are attended by men in plainer clothing. The strangers stand in the yard, with the servants behind them.

The servants are holding parcels wrapped in tapestries that must have traveled from palaces far away.

"They are from eastern lands," Joseph says to Mary and me. "Men who study the heavens. They have followed the new star that appeared around the time the baby was born."

I notice now that the neighbors have gathered, standing in small groups in the yard and at corners and doorways. They whisper to one another and stare at the visitors and look toward our open doorway at Mary and Joseph.

"What do they want?" Mary directs this to Joseph, whose expression is difficult to read.

"To pay homage."

She looks at him, her eyebrows high.

"They've come to worship the child, Mary."

Mary's breathing changes, much as it changed that night long ago when the angel appeared to her. Meanwhile, the strange group of men and servants are walking toward the small house, and Mary and Joseph back up as they enter the room. One of the men steps out from the group. He bows as he walks forward, hardly daring to meet Mary's eyes.

"Good lady, we mean no harm."

"Who told you about my son?"

Four or five others join the first man. I can see now that they aren't even from the same country. Their dress is not the same. The shades of their skin vary from soft beige to deep brown. And when the second man speaks, his accent is different from that of the first.

"We are astrologers," he says. "We study the stars and also the sacred writings of many places and peoples. And when the star appeared some time ago, we were compelled to follow it."

Another speaks. "When we began, we were not certain ourselves where the journey would end or what it would mean. But it has become clear to us that this child is marked by the heavens. In all our studies or dreams, nothing such as this has ever happened before. We are certain this child is God's anointed; he is the king of the Jews."

"Please." The first speaks again, motioning to the servants, who are still standing back. "We've brought gifts. They are hardly anything at all, but in this world they are precious. Please accept them on behalf of the child."

The servants come forward with their parcels. They place them on the ground and carefully unwrap them.

When the first tapestry is folded back, a box of dark wood appears. And as the astrologer lifts the lid, a reflection hits the air, and Mary gasps.

"This is gold, the treasure of kings. May he rule in peaceful times." The men, along with their servants, are on their knees now, and they bow to the floor.

The second parcel is unwrapped. Another man speaks. "Frankincense, an exquisite incense and worthy as the finest sacrifice. May his life be a fragrant offering to God."

A servant unwraps the third parcel, and another man speaks. "Myrrh, the most precious of anointing oils. May it preserve his health in life and his body in death."

Mary touches each gift, speechless. Only then does Joseph set the child down before the visitors. Jesus looks at them with interest. He moves forward a step while staying close to Mary, touching one of the boxes. The visitors gaze at him and bow low, their foreheads touching the floor, their rich clothing spread on the bare ground.

Slowly, reverently the visitors rise, along with their servants, and they go back outside and to the caravan. The camels bellow grumpily and rise, and the company comes to life. Then it continues down the road, and all of us watch, not knowing what to say.

As the caravan disappears, the neighbors' stares shift to us. They speak among themselves, apparently unwilling to approach Joseph or Mary. We return to the house, where the gifts, still surrounded by the tapestries, remain on the floor. It looks as if a king has ridden by and accidentally dropped some possessions. The colors and textures don't match the earthiness of this place.

Mary clings to her son while Joseph carefully repacks the boxes and wraps them in the cloths.

"What are you thinking?" I ask them both, because they don't act like people who have just been visited by rich strangers and left with gifts.

"I'm thinking that I have never seen so much wealth in one place," says Joseph. "The gold alone is a small fortune. The incense and myrrh as well. These are extravagant gifts." He looks somewhat worried, as if he's not sure how to take care of this sudden windfall.

"I'm thinking of what it means," Mary says softly. Jesus is on her lap, and he's definitely looking droopy, ready for that midafternoon nap. "The offering, the anointing."

"That, too," Joseph adds. "That, too. Each gift carries its own prophecy."

I wonder, then, what these particular parents dream for their son. How do they look forward? Do they imagine a daughter-in-law someday and grandchildren? Do they plan already for his inheritance? Have they considered sending him away to study, in Jerusalem perhaps, since he is to be a great leader of people, a man who will need to be educated and wise? Or would military duty be more appropriate? Wouldn't that experience be useful to a king?

"What will you do?" I look from one to the other.

"We'll keep these gifts in a safe place and wait until the

time comes for their use," Joseph says. Mary agrees. Sadness is in the angle of her head, the direction of her gaze.

"Even people from faraway lands know about your son," I say.

Mary is rocking little Jesus. His eyelids flutter to slits. His active arms and legs slow their motions.

"I knew that the star meant something." Joseph is gazing at his family. "I'm not trained to understand such things, but even a farmer or goatherd knows that a new star means something. I kept telling myself that I was imagining a connection between the star and Jesus. But I see it now. My imagination cannot begin to know what will be true for this child."

The next morning Jana was awakened by Aunt Cheryl tapping on her bedroom door.

"Mary Georgianna? Phone for you. Shall I have him call later?"

Him. If it was Dad, Aunt Cheryl would say so. And Dad had just called yesterday, so "him" could mean only one thing.

"I'll take it up here. Thanks."

Jana put on her robe and walked into the hallway as Aunt Cheryl headed downstairs. She picked up the phone on the little table under the family gallery.

"Hello?"

"Hey. How's it goin'? It's me."

Gary's greeting was always "Hey," as if "Hello" would require too much commitment or passion.

"Hi." Jana held the phone and searched for something to add to that.

"Merry Christmas," he said.

"Merry Christmas. You with your mom?"

"Yeah. Just thought I'd call."

Well, that was obvious.

"Why do you want to call?" She couldn't help it. He'd been such a jerk, why should she make this easy? Even so, her heart rate was too high for this early in the morning.

"Oh, you know."

"No, I don't know. Why call now, after—what—two months or something?"

She heard him sigh in that irritated way of his. "It hasn't been any two months."

"Well, we agreed that there are no strings attached. Nobody's obligated to stay in touch or anything like that. So I'm a little confused."

"I miss you, baby."

Now she sighed back and didn't answer.

"I mean, it's not that easy, just not seeing you anymore. I think we had some good things happening. What was so bad that you had to quit on me?"

She wished he'd just be quiet. The one thing that still made her weaken was Gary's voice—a velvety voice, a good voice for saying romantic things, for being a comfort, for leading her to bed.

"You just confuse me, Jana. I can't ever tell what you want."

"Maybe I don't know what I want. You don't seem to know what you want either. We're both just fumbling around. I need more direction."

"You've got direction. You just haven't found a good job yet. It's always like this between college and the rest of your life. And I'm doing okay too."

"Well, it got to where it didn't feel okay anymore. I don't know how else to explain it."

She'd been staring at her grandparents' wedding photo. Did they have direction, beyond making a living and having babies? It made her head hurt to try to imagine them at her age.

"Well, I just wanted to say Merry Christmas."

"Thanks, Gary. That was nice."

"Bye."

She went to the bathroom and directly into the shower. The hot spray felt good on her head and neck; she'd gotten tense while on the phone. That was part of the problem. Gary just made her tense. She wasn't sure why, but he did.

I never felt secure with him.

Was it something that basic and infantile? *Safety?* Did she actually want someone to *take care* of her? She stood in one position under the spray, allowing the hot water to hit her right on top of her head. In the heat and the steam she suddenly had an image of Joseph standing in the room with his family. He was putting away those extravagant gifts and saying that they would wait until they knew the right thing to do.

That's all your imagination, she said to herself. *Those were not real conversations. What do you want, some guy to lead you around on a donkey?*

No. I just want someone who has some conviction about his life. I want someone with inner stability. There's something about Gary that feels shaky to me.

"What would Gary do if God visited my life in some bizarre way?" She asked this aloud as she stepped out of the shower. She dried off and then rubbed a clear spot on the steamed-up mirror. Her face looked back at her, and it was more sorrowful than she expected. She knew that Gary would not understand what had happened to her in the living room night before last, that sudden awareness of Something Else in the moonlight. She wouldn't know how to talk to Gary about it. She hardly knew how to think about it herself. But as the steam cleared and she combed through her wet hair, she was a little relieved that Gary wasn't with her now. For part of the time he'd be a wonderful distraction, but he would not fit easily into most of what was going on here.

Unexpectedly, she shed some tears. Gary had made her feel so loved. He'd made her laugh, and they'd had some good times. She still couldn't imagine feeling so good with anyone again. But her life was opening up in strange ways, getting complex and demanding. She was on a huge journey, and Gary was not the traveling companion she needed.

*M*om came home in early afternoon. Despite all that her body had been through in the past twenty-four hours, her features were animated now. Jana couldn't tell if the energy behind her mother's look was enthusiasm because it was Christmas or sheer single-mindedness aimed at staying out of the hospital from now on. But Mom's eyes snapped just a little, and, of all things, she had glitter in her hair—lots of it. Her hair had been growing back steadily—at least she wasn't losing any more. But what little there was, was thin, and the way it had been styled created a holiday puffball effect. When Aunt Cheryl gave her a strange look, Mom said, "I asked Trish the nurse to do something with this pathetic little mop of mine. What do you think?"

"Stunning." Aunt Cheryl ventured a touch and then broke into giggles. "My gosh, how much hair spray did she use?"

"Enough that, if you want, you can hang ornaments in it."

When evening came, they gathered at the table for leftovers. A day's time hadn't hurt the flavor of anything. Mom still wasn't too hungry, but she took a little of everything, and she made sure the candles were lit.

"Mmmm. So glad I didn't waste my little appetite on hospital food today."

"You ate something, didn't you? This morning, at least?" Aunt Cheryl assumed the look of big sister taking charge again.

"I had some tea, some soupy hot cereal. They brought the lunch tray right at noon, and it looked so dismal, like something pretending to be a turkey dinner. I decided to hold out for the real thing."

They didn't talk much, other than Aunt Cheryl's recounting some of yesterday's dinnertime conversations. Chitchat. Jana felt alone suddenly. In two days she would leave, Mom would continue to live here, temporarily at least, and Jana would have life all to herself, to sort out, to live out. The prospect didn't feel wonderful at all.

After they cleared the dishes from the table, Aunt Cheryl held up her arms in the middle of the kitchen like a referee. "Forget doing dishes. We have presents to open." She led the way into the living room. Jana sat in the easy chair, Mom settled on the sofa, and Aunt Cheryl pulled up the footstool and sat near the tree. She passed out packages.

Mom and Aunt Cheryl were always great at gifts. They somehow knew the right color, the right size, the right *thing*. When Jana finished unwrapping her small pile of packages, she was surrounded by clothing, jewelry, and a book. Aunt Cheryl was completely impressed by the van Gogh reproduction Jana bought for her at the Art Institute. Mom gave a happy cry when she pulled out the soft green sweater and turtleneck set. She tapped the Marshall Fields box it came in. "You know what I like, don't you?" The earrings Jana had bought at an art fair were also well received by both women. The three of them sat back, surrounded by wrapping paper. Already it was dark outside. The tree lights gleamed, making the room feel warm.

"Okay, time for hot cider." Aunt Cheryl left them to go prepare dessert. Jana looked up to see Mom gazing at her. She appeared anxious.

"I have another gift for you," she said. "I'm not sure you'll like it though."

"I always like your gifts, Mom."

Mom didn't look convinced, but she pointed to a large unmarked box on the far side of the tree. "Okay. Go ahead."

Jana picked up the box, which wasn't as heavy as it looked. She sat on the sofa next to Mom and carefully peeled away the foil and ribbons. When she pulled apart the cardboard flaps, a musty smell met her.

"It's old stuff," Mom said. "Not worth anything, but I thought you might like it."

Several items were wrapped in tissue paper. Jana uncovered them, one by one:

> a paperweight made from a smooth river rock, with "Jesus
>   loves me" painted on it
> a small pin, edged in gold, which read "perfect attendance"
> a baptismal certificate
> shiny bookmarks with Bible verses on them
> a collage of words and phrases plastered together on a smooth
>   plaque: "trust, peace, thankfulness, obedience, joy"
> a white Bible with gold lettering on it: "The Holy Bible,"
>   and toward the bottom: "Della Irene Murray"

"Mom, this is your stuff." Jana looked at her mother, whose expression remained full of questions. "Why are you giving away your things?"

Maybe Mom and Aunt Cheryl had not been so honest about Mom's condition. Jana felt her world shift and everything go off balance.

"It's very specific stuff. I want you to have it because it represents something." Mom picked up each item and explained.

"The paperweight and the collage I made in Vacation Bible School. The bookmarks were prizes I won at church for memorizing Scripture verses. I was baptized and received this certificate when I was thirteen. The pin was for perfect attendance at Sunday school. The Bible was given to me by my parents when I was baptized." She held on to the Bible, touching the gold lettering of her name. "It's the story of my faith, the faith I had as a child."

Jana took the Bible. The white cover had yellowed some. "Why do you want me to have these things?"

"Because I didn't give you anything else in your whole life that was as important as this. By the time you were born, I had thrown my faith away. I thought I'd outgrown it. And I didn't want to force it on my daughter. I thought I was being liberated, progressive, whatever. That's the way we thought back then."

Jana was quiet. She understood that the look on her mom's face was pain. Regret. "Mom, I'm okay."

"No, you're not okay. You're grown-up now, but the one thing I should have given you I didn't. And what we believe when we're young—it's important. Do you see that?"

"But is it more important than what you believe now?"

Mom's eyes were getting misty. "Well, now I believe what I did back then, only now I believe as a grownup. It's different, but it's not. What I've discovered is that it's all true, truer than when it was just a story I memorized for a bookmark prize in Sunday-school class."

"I'm glad your faith helps you now."

"It's more than that, Mary Georgianna. I know you think I've turned religious because I need extra support to get through all this stuff. But the God I left back then never left me. And cancer or no cancer, I'm not going to neglect my soul anymore."

Mom seemed so desperate for Jana to understand.

"I know, Mom."

"Not really. Not the way you'd know if I hadn't been trying to be this self-sufficient hero-mom who didn't need religion."

"You gave me yourself, and you still do."

"But I won't always be here. And Dad won't either. There has to be more. There has to be faith."

Jana returned the Bible to the box. "Maybe I have faith too. Maybe God has been looking out for me in other ways."

"Oh, I hope so." Mom examined the painted river rock before placing it back in the box.

"Mom, I don't want these things, because they're yours. Keep them here, and leave them to me eventually, but don't make me take them now, okay?"

"I guess they don't really mean anything, do they? I hoped they might wake up something, but they're my memories, not yours."

"It does mean something." The despair on Mom's face made Jana search for something else to say. "It's like the gifts the wise men brought Jesus. Each gift had its own prophecy for Jesus' life."

Mom looked at her in surprise. "Yes, I suppose it did."

"The gold meant that he was the King of kings. The frankincense foretold how his life would be an offering to God, and the myrrh—"

She didn't expect the sudden pressure in her chest. The time to be weepy was last night, when Mom was in the hospital and the house was so deathly quiet. But her throat hurt now, and she couldn't say any more.

"The myrrh foretold his awful death." Mom's face turned calm, her words a whisper.

"I think that Mary was sad when she opened that box." Jana swiped at a tear that went running down her face without permission.

"But she opened it, didn't she? And she kept those gifts." Mom placed the box on Jana's lap. "I'm giving you my whole life in this box, sweetheart. It includes death, but more than that. And anyway"—she stopped to wipe her eyes—"if I can't give it to you until I'm dead, then it could be years and years."

Jana set the box aside and wrapped Mom in a hug. She cried a little, but mainly she breathed deeply, to take in all of Mom, even the hospital smells, even the soft shudders of Mom's tears.

"Merry Christmas, baby."

"Merry Christmas, Mom."

I go to visit them the next day. I want to see them, I want to play with Jesus, and I want to look again at the fantastic gifts that are stored safely in a corner cupboard.

When I come to the door, it's open, and I see a pile of things in the center of the room. Someone touches my shoulder from behind. It's Joseph, carrying large empty sacks. He greets me and hurries past. Mary appears then, things bundled in her arms. I hear Jesus singing an unintelligible child's song. He is tapping a large pottery bowl with a wooden spoon, grinning at the noise.

"What's happening?" I ask.

Mary stops, her face a blur of emotions. "We're leaving."

"Why?"

She comes up to me, and her words are quick and quiet. "Herod heard about Jesus—from the men who brought the gifts. Only they didn't know at the time what Herod's intentions were. But an angel—" She puts a hand to her mouth, her expression crumpling, and tears stream over her fingers. I put my arm around her. She shakes her head and sniffles. "An angel came to Joseph in a dream last night. If Herod finds our son, he'll kill him. So we're going to Egypt." She puts a finger on my mouth. "No one knows where we're going. Only you. Please, you can't tell anyone, no matter who it is."

I help them pack. They shut the doors and windows as they work, afraid the neighbors will figure out what's happening. Poor Mary—Mary who has adopted this Bethlehem community. _Why doesn't any place feel like home anymore?_ She can trust no one. First she lost her family and place in Nazareth, now this. She doesn't cry again because she's too busy. I look after Jesus, who is unruffled by all this activity.

At evening we share a meal, likely the last hot one they will have for days. They will go once it's dark. They will leave town the way they arrived, with one donkey and as many provisions as it can carry. I see Joseph tuck the gold into a pouch and put it around his neck and under his clothes. It seems they will need this gift sooner than expected.

Tonight there is just a sliver of moon, but the black sky is filled with stars. It's become my habit to locate the new star, the one that has changed everything, the star that has stirred up madness and murder in a king who otherwise would take no interest in a common carpenter and his wife and son.

We leave town by the quietest, most deserted streets. Fortunately, little Jesus is sound asleep, contained in a wide sling that crosses Joseph's stomach and chest. Just his little legs are hanging out. I walk with them for nearly two miles. We come to the crest of a hill. Looking back, we see sleeping

Bethlehem, its handful of lights glittering like ornaments. Ahead of us are darkness and hill after hill. A single, swinging light off to the south and close to the ground gives evidence of a shepherd, his flock a dark knot against the pale, rocky ground. We don't say anything, but the three of us are remembering those other shepherds, that other night, our first night in the village now receding behind us in the silence.

We hug in the dark. Even Joseph cries. I don't think it's because he'll miss me so much or even Bethlehem. He cries for the treacherous time, for the days ahead, and the long hours of hoping and trying and not knowing.

I think I will hold on to Mary for the rest of my life. She still seems so young to me, just a girl who finds herself in the center of a plot that stretches beyond this time and place.

I watch her walk away. Her back is straight, and she grasps Joseph's arm. They walk beside the donkey, which is loaded with the sum of their earthly possessions. Mary is a refugee, her little son a fugitive. Her husband will stay beside them, even if it means dying to protect them. They are their own small society, a mystical trio that in some strange way stands between earth and heaven.

I watch them leave, and I cry. I cannot move, even when Mary glances back and smiles. She knows that on another day I will appear on her pathway again. I know it too. Because now I have an interest in this baby. In the middle of

*my own life, far from this time and place, I have pinned my
hopes upon the Christ child. And I will walk with him many
times before my own journey is through.*

Jana dried her eyes and closed the journal. She placed it,
with her mother's Bible, on the dresser. These were her possessions, or perhaps they possessed her. At the very least they were
gifts, and she felt certain that they would wisely and wonder-
fully shape her life. For the first time in a long time she had
true hope—of stepping into her very own future, of prophecies
waiting to come true.

ABOUT THE AUTHOR

Vinita Hampton Wright has been a book editor for thirteen years. She writes fiction and nonfiction and is a facilitator of workshops on creativity and writing. When not dealing with written words, she is walking the Chicago lakefront, inventing meals for friends, watching as many films as she can, and making a good life with her husband, Jim, and her needy canine, Nala.

The Soul Tells a Story
Writing from Your Creative/Spiritual Heart
—a writer's workshop led by Vinita Hampton Wright

This workshop is designed to explore creativity and spirituality, especially in the writing life. Topics include: discovering your creative gifts, learning about the creative process, building a healthy writing life, finding the support you need, tapping creativity from all aspects of your life, and recognizing how the creative and spiritual intersect. Ms. Wright designs each workshop according to the makeup of its participants. For more information, write to

Vinita Hampton Wright
5338 S. Greenwood Ave., #3
Chicago, IL 60615
or call
773-363-4496

Also by Vinita Hampton Wright

Grace at Bender Springs
Velma Still Cooks in Leeway

To learn more about WaterBrook Press and view
our catalog of products, log on to our Web site:
www.waterbrookpress.com

WATERBROOK
PRESS